Police Rescue 2

Bill Green has worked as a print and television journalist in Australia and North America and has filed
stories from China, South-East Asia and Mexico. He
has been an investigative journalist and crime reporter in Australia and North America. His screenplay of
Freud and the Nazis Go Surfing has been sold to Village
Roadshow and Island Pictures, and was shortlisted
for workshopping with Robert Redford's Sundance
Institute.

Police Rescue 2
BILL GREEN

Mandarin

A Mandarin Paperback
POLICE RESCUE 2

First published in Great Britain 1993
by Mandarin Paperbacks
an imprint of Reed Consumer Books Ltd
Michelin House, 81 Fulham Road, London SW3 6RB
and Auckland, Melbourne, Singapore and Toronto

Copyright © Southern Star Xanadu 1992

ISBN 0 7493 1550 4

A CIP catalogue record for this title
is available from the British Library

Printed and bound in Great Britain
by Cox & Wyman Ltd, Reading, Berks

One

Sergeant Peter Ridgeway thought he had adjusted to being discarded. His life away from the ambitious major squads had become something of a delight. The skills he had learned in Special Operations were easily applied to the needs of Police Rescue, and there were none of the dirty adrenalin hits that turned you from a human being into a fearful killing machine. Rescue helped people, no matter who they might be. It was good not to have to calculate your reactions to people and circumstances. You were allowed to be generous with your skills.

Ridgy had been part of the occasional and casual murder of Special Operations. Their speciality was the violent raid. They shot first and covered it all up later. He was glad that horror stuff was all behind him.

For years he hadn't regarded himself as a discard, a reject, a time server. But now, in the space of a week, it had all caught up with him.

It began when Gina Alvarez walked into the squad room to take up a position as Inspector Adams's secretary. After years of being satisfied with his life Ridgy began attempting to measure himself as a man again. He knew it was ridiculous, knew nothing would come of it, but the process started up anyway.

Gina was certainly not the sort of woman that Ridgy had ever regarded as available to him, but he recognised he was jealous of Mickey and Angel in their casual assumption that it would be either one of them she would fall for.

Gina had a lushness about her; that was the only way Ridgy could describe it. Everything about her was exaggerated. Her lips were not only large and tremulous, the curves of them were deep and long. She was tall, about Ridgy's height, and her legs were incredibly long. And although she was slim, she could never have been thought of as thin.

Damn it, Ridgy thought on those occasions he caught her passing presence, her clothes are always tight.

His eyes would follow her involuntarily. Several times as she strode out of his vision he found his eyes locked into those of Inspector Adams. The inspector's eyes were accusing. Come on, mate, they said, that's a young woman you're staring at: you're too old to be fooled by this stuff. Yeah, Ridgy thought, and what about you? Hell, you hired her.

Gina's arrival coincided with a request from Ridgy's old squad for Police Rescue to back them up in a raid on the mansion of a notorious and well-connected crim, Vic Wilson.

Ridgy was against joining forces with the thugs he knew. They were into ultimate violence and would risk themselves in any confrontation, just to gain a few seconds. Adams told him working with Special Operations was good public relations for Rescue, that occasionally helping out serious people built up their survival credits.

2

Ridgy's job was to brief the rest of the squad and liaise with Special Operations. In preparing his brief he found himself calculating that Gina would hear it, and he put in more work than he usually would have undertaken.

The key members of the Police Rescue squad were there at the briefing. Mickey, the short, handsome and muscular one, who was a vital component of any hazardous rescue work. He was a smart-arse but totally reliable under pressure. He had been a good friend to Ridgy for some years now, and each trusted the other's judgements in crisis situations. There was Georgia Rattray, an attractively tough woman in her early thirties. She had come from vice, and had out-parried all the men in the squad who had regarded her as a potential weak link in their operations. She and Gina immediately discovered a camaraderie and a sense of humour sharp enough to exclude the males of the squad. They just weren't fast enough.

Frog was the stalwart of the group. He always had an alternative method up his sleeve if all else failed. He was a good-natured fellow, and had been a spirit-ed campaigner for justice in many squads before being given to Rescue, where his politicking, he recognised, was out of place. That was a disappoint-ment to him.

Angel had been on the streets before coming to the force. His knowledge of petty crime was immense, but he had finally chosen Rescue to get away from the temptations involved in the work of the other squads. He was obsessed with his style, clothes, and his ability to match Mickey at various tasks.

Then there was Sootie, who could dismantle a car

in seconds—and not just cars either, and Ptomaine, the travelling supplier of food on all occasions, who could throw in his weight at the sites of major rescues when more hands were needed. Ptomaine was the butt of tireless jokes about food quality in the canteen.

And Inspector Adams was there. He looked after the squad's administration and morale, but was mainly seen as an encumbrance by the stars of the squad. And, of course, Gina.

Ridgy saw when he began his spiel to the assembled squad, that Gina was taking dictation from the inspector in his glass-bound office. She might see him, but she wouldn't hear him. Anyway, he was glad he had put in the extra work because the draft of the talk he had committed to memory was larded with considerable humour.

He stood to the side of the screen placed in front of the notice board and operated the slide projector with a remote control.

The surveillance shots of Vic Wilson showed a thick, muscular man in his forties. He had a brutal energy about him, and a sharp piercing glance. He was a man aware of his environment at all times.

Ridgy understood how incredibly good the photographer had been. He had got in close and hadn't been seen. 'All right you mob,' he said to the assembled company. 'This bloke probably needs no introduction, but meet Vic Wilson.

'At forty-two, our Mr Wilson is best known as a racing identity. But his interest in fast horses hasn't stopped him becoming interested in prostitution, protection, and illegal casinos.'

The group were riveted by a shot of Wilson in

confrontation with an Asian man on a small point of land that jutted out from the otherwise sandy beach at Mosman. 'More recently,' Ridgy continued, 'he has entered the main game in town—heroin.

'You'll remember Mr Trang from last year.' The surveillance shot showed Wilson slapping Trang's face. 'He's unfortunately no longer a player.'

'Ah ha,' Sootie began, 'food poisoning was it?' The group laughed.

'Actually it was lead poisoning, Senior Constable Coledale, and we're not talking Taiwanese saucepans here. Wilson is not to be underestimated—and I know I'm not telling you anything new—but what I am saying is that nothing of this operation should be mentioned to friends. Don't run off the mouth at the local boozer. Wilson is dangerous because he's a hands-on operator. He likes to kill, and he's good at it. The people he employs are good, and they're loyal—to him. They won't hesitate to shoot. That's our information, anyhow, and I think we should take it to heart.

'Now, I'd like you to meet Senior Sergeant Travis from the Special Operations team.'

Travis stepped forward into the light close to the projector. He was tough. This bloke had been aged by exercise. He was so fit the skin of his youth was now in folds where the fat had been extracted by an iron will on the obstacle courses of a myriad training grounds. His eyes were slits, their impassiveness lent them an unbelieving quality.

'Besides these aforementioned dealings,' Travis said, his voice sharp and challenging, 'Wilson also has a number of legit businesses. Restaurants, hotels, car yards. But he's probably best known as a bookie.'

The Wilson mansion appeared on screen. Its fortress-like architecture was impressive. 'This is his Achilles heel,' Travis said. 'Our information is that Wilson is using his bookmaking operations to launder money. According to the Police Intelligence unit, he receives huge amounts of money which he whacks through his books. It comes out as winnings and he takes twenty per cent.'

'How can they work that?' Mickey called from the side of the room where he was lounging with Angel, watching Gina through the glass of Adams's office.

'Easy,' Travis said. 'They have two sets of books. One for the racetrack, and one for after the track. They simply take the books back to this mansion here, and rewrite the taking and paying out of winning bets.'

'Yeah,' Mickey said doubtfully. 'But the board of stewards can seize those books at the track. They do it if some horse has run badly. They trace the bets; see what sort of influence is behind the run.'

'That's fine. It does happen occasionally. They show the genuine books, and the money can't be laundered that day. But in practice the board of stewards is calling for those books less and less these days.'

Ridgy saw a vision of Gina walking towards him. She was smiling at someone. It appeared to be directed at him. He certainly didn't feel he'd done anything to deserve a smile that was so profuse. He hardly knew her. He was unaware of the effect a beautiful woman has on the people on whom she chooses to smile. He had never been on the receiving end before. Often the woman too doesn't know the effect of her presence. Not to start with anyway. She just smiles like

6

anyone else, and the results can be devastating.

'Excuse me, Sergeant,' Gina said to him. 'These are for you.' She gave him a bundle of files.

'Aah, good,' Ridgy said. 'Thanks.'

'Hey,' he heard Mickey say to Angel. 'I might borrow those files from Ridgy.'

'It's underwear, not files you're supposed to borrow,' Angel said.

Travis had been silent for several moments, but no-one had noticed. 'Are you blokes all quite finished?' he said. 'Now, if we can grab Wilson and his books, we've got a dead set chance of pinning Lloyd Prosser, the Dayton brothers and George Cravoni.'

The squad looked impressed. 'That's right. We're not talking reserve grade here.'

Ridgy took over narrating Wilson's biography as the surveillance shots continued. Wilson was in the street with a woman who looked older than him. 'As you would imagine for a man of Mr Wilson's style, he has a wife. Vic makes sure Mrs Wilson's away overseas a lot and she's smart enough not to ask any questions about his wanderings and his appetites.'

The scene changed again. Wilson was sitting by a swimming pool with an attractive young woman. 'Meet Annie Fowler,' Ridgy continued, 'twenty-five, known till recently as a dancer in one of Mr Wilson's establishments.'

The harmless Romeo of Rescue, Sootie, called out, 'Can't we get any closer?'

Annie Fowler was seen in closer and closer close-ups as if on Sootie's demand. She was fulfilling Wilson's fantasy of how a sexually demented nymphomaniac should look. Obviously Sootie's fantasy

7

as well. She had obviously been filmed for the pleasure of the Intelligence unit by a prurient photographer.

'Is that how you like it, Sootie?' Ridgy asked.

'I reckon. Hey, how do you, er, join the Police Intelligence unit?'

Mickey laughed. 'By passing an intelligence test, Sootie.'

'Counts you out, Sootie,' Georgia said.

The next shot was of Annie Fowler in a hospital bed, badly bruised. 'God,' Georgia said. 'No-one deserves that.'

'Yeah,' Ridgy said. 'I'd anticipated a bit of levity at this point. So I felt I needed to remind you of who you're dealing with. These people in the shots coming up, were all known associates of Vic Wilson. I stress, were.'

There were some tough men in suits getting in and out of large cars, a few women in evening finery.

The shots changed to the house again, roving over the building, the expansive garden, the fences and the iron gates. 'Now this is where we come in.' Ridgy looked across at Travis.

Travis looked around the faces in front of him, and he felt they needed geeing up. These people weren't hot for pursuit like his own men, they were laid-back, in need of inspiring.

'We need to grab Wilson exactly at the time he's putting the phantom bets into the ledgers.' He looked around to emphasise the point, and tapped the screen with a pointer. It moved under the touch. 'All the information we need is in those sets of books. We understand the stuff is also duplicated on computer.'

He looked directly at Mickey and Angel and Sootie. 'We need you blokes to get us in there.'

Frog, with that hefty calmness of demeanour capable of unsettling all plans with a direct appeal to common sense, began his questioning. 'Why us? Thought you blokes were the door-breaking experts.'

'You blokes have got the equipment,' Travis said.

'How much time have we got?' Frog asked.

'We'll come to that.'

'Are you covering us while we do this work?'

'Yes.'

'We could show you how to use the stuff, no trouble,' Frog said.

'You blokes are the skilled ones. You would seem to be the best choice.'

'That's right,' Mickey said. 'But the rest is bullshit.'

'What are you saying?' Travis asked.

'You blokes had a go at getting in a month ago and you couldn't do it. You're desperate for us. Your mob haven't been trained properly.'

Travis wasn't used to the irreverence. He demanded sycophants in his squad; blokes who would kill when ordered without hesitation; blokes who respected those who gave the orders. He demanded slavishness. His voice was low and accusing when he spoke to Mickey. 'That was a covert operation, Sergeant. How did you find out about it?'

'How do you reckon?'

'I'm asking.'

'We're coppers too, mate.'

'Yeah, well I'll see about that.'

Ridgy put his hand on Travis's sleeve. 'Now, come

on mate, your blokes are so gung-ho they can't help letting off steam in the first pub they go into. They tell everyone, you know that.'

'By Jesus, they won't in future,' Travis said.

Ridgy saw Gina look at him. It was just a passing glance, but he was glad she had seen him relaxed, dealing with a problem that could have become major. And it was not as if he wanted anything more than respect. He could be friends with her.

After Ridgy saw Travis off the base he went looking for Mickey. He found him with Frog, both agreeing to be indignant and angry over this job with the Special Operations team. 'What the hell is this all about?' Ridgy asked.

Mickey was eager to get out of the job. 'Ridgy, those bloody blokes just want us to do their job for them.'

'So what, for Christ's sake?'

'Hey, they're a bunch of cowboys, you know that. They're pricks and they're nasty. Why do we have to hold their bloody hands?'

'Listen, Travis was spot on. Police regulations say we do the big break-ins.'

'Yeah, they stuff up first, *then* they stick to regulations,' Frog said.

'Hey, come on, Frog, what's eating you?' Ridgy was unused to Frog voicing an opinion on anything other than a practical way to approach an unusual rescue operation.

Frog wasn't to be denied with a rhetorical question though. 'I tell ya what, I'm sick of the bloody force. It's run by a pack of bandits on the take, or these homicidal dippies from Special Operations.'

'Jesus, Frog, what are you talking about, mate?' said Ridgy.

Mickey, too, was surprised by Frog's vehemence. 'Hey, I wouldn't go as far as that,' he countered.

'Listen, Mickey. How do you think bastards like Wilson exist? Because they're protected all the way along the line by their political mates, or our senior blokes. That's how this city operates. These days you're not socially acceptable unless you're a bloody big-time crim.'

Mickey was anxious to capitalise on the outburst, shaft the knowledge home to Ridgy so that something constructive could be done on the operation. 'OK, so we're helping them. But not on what they give us. All it takes is someone white-anting at Special Ops and we miss vital stuff. You know, we get there and the walls and the gates have just been juiced with an electrical circuit and the place is impregnable. Junk like that.'

'Right,' Ridgy said. 'We do our own reconnaissance.'

*   *   *

The Wilson house would be a problem. That was obvious at first glance. There were dogs, cameras, a high wall, and scenic lights that would flood the area at the first indication there was a false move in the grounds. The garden had been designed to give no cover for thirty metres around the house. The only weakness was the swimming-pool fence. The fence could give a reasonable sort of camouflage, purely because the eye tends to rest on the first object it sees and not naturally penetrate further. Anyone looking from the house would be tricked by that unless they were very experienced. The pool itself was up close to the side of the house.

Mickey kept up a barrage of complaint as he and Ridgy took shots from their plumber's van.

'Hey, Mickey,' Ridgy said. 'You can't leave anything alone, once it's rattling your bloody brain pan.'

Mickey was persistent because Ridgy's answer might give him some insight as to why he, Mickey, tended to obey people on things he didn't always agree with. If he could see how it was for Ridgy perhaps he would see it in himself, and learn how to deal with it.

He had seriously tried to explain to Ridgy why he was behaving in this way. 'I can't understand why you're sticking up for those mongrels after what they did to you.'

'They didn't do anything to me, mate. I requested a transfer because I wanted out. That's all.'

'Yeah, but they pushed you.'

'Look, Mickey. I wanted to get out. I didn't want to be in the position of pulling the trigger on some poor bugger again.'

'Hey, come on, the inquiry backed you up.'

'That's paperwork. I shot him, Mick. Now just forget it will ya? Leave it alone. There are times on the job when I forget it. I'd like to now. The rest of the time it's with me, OK? If you kill someone it stays with you. It comes back to you when you're feeling good, bad, anytime. Some of those blokes back from 'Nam, they know about it now. It can turn you bananas.'

Mickey nodded towards the other side of the property. 'There's something on the wall of the pool.

You're taller than me. I'll bunk you and you snap.'

Ridgy's foot was resting in Mickey's hands as if in a stirrup. 'A bit higher,' Ridgy said from close to the top of the wall. It was at that moment they were hit from behind. Mickey, stunned, sank to his knees. His vision appeared to be operating in slow motion. Ridgy had jumped down from the wall, but he was held from behind. The attackers imagined Mickey was out of it and turned to Ridgy, slamming him up against the bricks. But Ridgy twisted quickly and caught one in the groin. Mickey summoned consciousness and threw himself on the nearest bloke, trying to sink his teeth into the neck. Strength seeps last from the jaw. He found his mouth full of leather coat.

He was fully conscious moments later and was driving himself forward with his knees and elbows, a close-in attack style all his own, when Ridgy said, 'Donnelly.'

'Ridgeway,' the taller attacker said.

All four looked shamefaced. It was lucky no-one was there to snap a shot of coppers attacking coppers. Of course you could never be sure. It would only take a bored and curious housewife with a video in these wealthy suburbs and the altercation would be on the evening news.

Donnelly, the tall dark bloke, offered an explanation. 'We're on reconnaissance ourselves.'

'What the hell did you jump us for?' Ridgy asked. Mickey thought he saw Donnelly's eyes shift too much. 'Sorry fellas. We thought you were Wilson's opposition. There's always someone trying to knock him off. We want him for ourselves.'

'Really,' Mickey said.

'Yeah, if he so much as flicks an eyelash Saturday, it's goodnight, Vic,' Donnelly said.

'Yeah, that sounds like you blokes,' Mickey said.

'OK, see you around,' Donnelly said.

Watching them go Mickey said, 'What the hell were they up to? Are they into protecting Wilson or what? There's something weird about them getting into us like that.'

Crossing the road to the plumber's van, Ridgy said, 'Did you see those blokes in the limo?'

'No.'

'They went past the house while we were talking. It was those developers who did the Victoria Street stuff. You know, someone did them a favour and the woman disappeared.'

'The woman who was leading the campaign against the development?'

'Yeah.'

'Nice neighbourhood.'

'Yeah,' Ridgy said. 'They were slowing until they saw us.'

Two

Ridgy found himself trying to manufacture reasons for leaving the base. Oh, he appreciated Gina's presence, but he wanted to place himself out of danger. When he realised how he was feeling, he laughed. There was no way he would sexually harass anyone. Only, he was uneasy with Gina around. He wanted to talk to her, and he couldn't do it without revealing how he felt about her. He had no experience with small talk. To begin talking to her would be dangerous. He ridiculed this thought. The jobs he'd had in the force had all been of the hazardous variety. But this was a different fear, much worse. He might have to change his behaviour; respond to her presence. It was ridiculous that someone of his size, age and experience could be frightened of a woman who was probably half his weight and, if he had just a few more years under his belt, was young enough to be his daughter. But that's human behaviour for you, and he understood that it was never simple.

He felt guilty about sneaking away from base. He would have liked to have gone home at lunch times to think things through, but Mickey, who had only a few months ago separated from his wife, Des, was staying with him now, and he didn't want Mickey to find him mooching around.

He liked to think that Gina liked being around him, although he had absolutely no evidence of that.

If I'm wrong about that, he thought, I can certainly understand how men begin approaching women in the work place. Not that he would have ever done that. He knew how men deluded themselves. He had seen too much of it. What some men thought was good fine instinct was often poorly timed lust.

Around knock-off time Mickey caught up with Ridgy. 'Let's go and see Gina's band tonight,' he said.

'Her band? What are you talking about?'

'She's a singer, mate. Got a great gig at the Charnel House. Well, she tells me it's pretty good.'

'What kind of music?'

'Whatever kind they play.'

'Aah, I dunno.'

'Come on, Ridgy. I'm going anyway. Plus I got a bit of a wager on with Angel.'

'On her?'

'Yeah.'

The decision was made for Ridgy. He would protect her from these two predators.

'One thing though, mate,' Mickey said. 'You don't mind if I bring her home?'

'You blokes,' Ridgy said, shaking his head. 'No, Mickey, you go for it.'

'Thanks mate.'

'One thing though.'

'Yeah?'

'Could I get ten bucks on Angel?'

Mickey laughed.

Georgia was walking past and, overhearing, said,

'You might find she has taste, Mickey.' It stopped Mickey, but he didn't apply any meaning to it other than that she was pointing out an aspect to be considered. 'Yeah,' he said seriously. 'She probably has.' Ridgy walked off smiling.

Mickey was about to follow him when Georgia stopped him with a hand. 'What's up with you?' she said. 'All day I've heard you sounding off over the Special Operations mob.'

Mickey flicked through the roster. 'Guns are not our job,' he said.

'But we can handle them,' Georgia said.

'We can't always. No-one can always. There's always the mistake. Ridgy was in Special Ops. He shot the wrong person . . . by mistake. An innocent bloke. Not his fault. The bloke just happened to be there at the wrong time and someone yelled he had a gun. That's how easily all this stuff can go wrong.'

Georgia looked directly into Mickey's face. The gaze was confrontational. 'A lot of other things can go wrong just as easily,' she said.

Mickey knew exactly what she was talking about. 'Georgia we agreed we would cool it, that we wouldn't tie each other down. We'd be friends.'

'That's fine. But chasing after young girls as if you're still an irresponsible kid is another. Do you understand?'

'Hey, trust me,' Mickey said. 'I'm not that old. It's just that my work has made me look . . . more mature.' He was laughing at her.

'I trust you about as far as I could kick a bag of spuds.'

Mickey grinned. 'You know, it's when you say stuff like that I realise you're a naive country girl at heart.'

'Get lost,' Georgia said.

* * *

Mickey's preparation for his night out with Ridgy and later—he hoped—with Gina was to gaze at his good-looking dial in the bathroom mirror for a good minute. This wasn't a ritual. This was serious examination. Would a young woman like Gina find him attractive? His eyes examined each portion of his face. If it wasn't for the deepening crowsfeet at the outer edge of each eye he might pass for twenty-eight. The rest of his skin was tanned, tight, and, he had to admit, pretty well moulded. He smiled at himself in the glass and wobbled his head the way a clown might. He was sending himself up . . . a little. Ridgy caught him at it when he poked his head in the bathroom door to hurry him up. 'Jesus!' he exclaimed. 'You've got some hope,' he added with mock sarcasm.

The club was crowded when they got there, the musicians still tuning up their electronic gear. As they made their way to a table it started. BLAM! The drums sounded out with the first wild chords from the guitars and Gina bounded onto the stage like a cat. How can she move with such style in high heels? Ridgy wondered. Her voice was quick with the beat, and husky. She moaned and tossed her notes. Jazz, thought Ridgy. I didn't know I'd like it so much.

She's only a kid, Mickey thought. How can she sing so well? How does she know how to move like that? He felt the stirrings of inadequacy. Her thighs might be slim and delightful, but to dance with such

18

strength ... Wow, he whispered to himself.

'Hey,' he said suddenly to Ridgy. 'What's that little grub doing here?' He pointed through the crowd to Angel, moving to the bar.

'Same as you,' Ridgy said. 'Remember?'

Angel caught sight of them and joined them. 'What are you doing here?'

'What do you reckon?' Mickey answered.

The lustful trio watched and listened to their squad secretary perform as well as any rock star. Her gyrations were not just those of an acrobat warming up, what she was doing was something far more interesting. Outrageous, but she was also holding something back. There was something softer there than just the wild display. And then it was over.

The trio were spellbound, the absence of the music only gradually releasing them from the performance.

'Wow!' Angel said. Mickey leaned forward to say something, but saw Gina approaching out of the corner of his eye, and began smiling broadly. Angel wondered about this rapid change of demeanour and followed Mickey's glance. He shook his head at her, smiling. 'That was unbelievable,' he said to her.

'Hi guys,' she said. Ridgy realised it wouldn't have sounded right for her to say, 'G'day, yous blokes.'

'Top performance,' Mickey said.

'What did you think, Ridgy?' Gina asked as she sat down.

'Good,' Ridgy said, feeling awkward. Expansive language wasn't his forte, and he wasn't sure what it was he had enjoyed, beyond watching Gina move. 'Good,' he said, this time giving more emphasis to the word.

'How about a drink?' Angel said.

'Yeah,' Gina said.

'I'll get it,' Mickey said, rising, wondering where this sudden gallantry had come from.

'I'll help you,' Angel said, needing to remove himself from Gina's presence while his mind adjusted to this new perception of her.

Gina smiled at Ridgy. 'They're just kids aren't they.'

'In some ways,' Ridgy answered. 'Women are a problem for them. They've got to prove themselves all the time.' I'm doing a pretty good job of demolishing them, Ridgy thought. They won't be succeeding with her.

'It's great you came down,' Gina said to him, and then she touched his tie quickly. 'Like the tie.'

'I'm glad I came,' Ridgy said. 'I haven't been out much since my marriage bit the dust. It's a new sort of night life going on these days.'

Mickey turned from the bar and saw Ridgy and Gina through the crowd. There was a definite intimacy about them. He nudged Angel and nodded in their direction. 'Hey, what do you reckon?' he said.

'Wouldn't have believed it,' said Angel.

Back at the table during the next set they watched Gina singing directly to Ridgy.

'I reckoned all the time she was a bit pushy,' Angel called out against the music.

Mickey nodded. 'Yeah, never could stand that in a woman.'

'She's an entertainer, guys,' Ridgy said. 'That's how they are, always up front. It frightens some people.'

Mickey yelled at Ridgy. 'Since when did you know

all this? You've been hiding it, mate.'

Ridgy smiled enigmatically. 'Takes understanding fellas. You know: if you know people you understand what's going on; what they're like. I've always had a good instinct that way.'

'Yeah, well I'm shooting through,' Mickey said. 'Never liked this sort of music anyway.'

'I'll come with you mate.'

The two foiled Romeos made their way through the crowd out to the car park.

'Jeeze, Ridgy! Can you believe it?' Angel said.

'The bastard always was a bit of a sly one,' Mickey said.

'Sly,' Angel exclaimed. 'He just looked at her and she fell over.'

'Yeah.'

'You're gonna have to brush up on the old technique,' Angel said.

'You know what he said to me once? I never took any notice, you know, I figured he was an old bugger just sounding off.'

'Yeah, what did he say?'

'He said, "The technique is that there is no technique."'

'What the hell does that mean?'

'Dunno, but looks like it works.'

'Yeah, well she'll keep his mind off Saturday. He'll be calm, all blissed out . . . the bastard.'

Mickey was going to tell Angel the doubts he had about Saturday's raid. If Wilson was in with those big-time developers who had seen them at the gates they would have alerted him—unless they thought the four of them had been Wilson's security. Yeah, and what if Special Operations was looking after Wilson? He didn't want to go into it. The politics could be really bloody murky. Maybe it was graft and corruption. Maybe the raid was only a face-saver or something. But he decided against telling Angel because he was really only a kid, and he still thought the force was something terrific. And Mickey was pissed off at the moment too, and didn't feel too friendly towards anyone.

The two of them split up at the car park and headed for different haunts. At least, Mickey pretended he had somewhere else to go, but he ended up sitting in front of the television, disgruntled and in a critical mood. The television was showing junk. No old movies.

He woke to find Ridgy in the room, alone.

'Good movie was it, mate?'

'Bloody awful. How did you go?'

'Well, um.'

'Did you take her home or anything?'

'No.'

Mickey became triumphant. 'Aah mate, you're getting old. A woman like that and all you want to do is—'

The hall door opened and Gina walked in. 'Hi, Mickey,' she said. Mickey wondered why he was constantly being caught out. It didn't happen to other people all the time, did it?

'Coffee?' Ridgy asked Gina.

'No thanks,' Gina said, smiling, and she inclined her head towards another room in the house. She headed off and Ridgy followed.

'I wouldn't mind a coffee,' Mickey said lamely as Ridgy closed the door behind them.

Three

Inspector Adams ran into Ridgy outside his office. He thought Ridgy's mouth seemed slack and his eyes unfocused. 'Jesus, what's wrong with you?' he asked. 'Have you got the flu?' He examined Ridgy's face with some distaste. 'Get home, mate,' he added. 'Look after yourself.'

Ridgy smiled. 'Never felt better.'

Sootie walked behind the two of them. 'Quiet night then, Ridgy?' Adams looked irritated by the comment and walked off, and Ridgy scowled at Mickey as they walked into the canteen. 'Hey,' Mickey said. 'I didn't say a thing.'

'Hi,' Gina said, as she walked through the room, looking at Mickey with mocking eyes.

'Hi,' Ridgy said, and then whispered as he turned, 'What a great night.'

The squad had settled down by the time Travis from Special Operations arrived to brief them again.

Travis walked and talked like an army type. It was all strategy and logistics and time. The time factor worried Mickey.

'You've got two minutes to get us in there,' Travis said.

'Starting from when?' Mickey asked.

'Starting from the moment we first hit the place.'

'Why only two minutes?'

'Once he knows we're on our way in, any more than two minutes and he'll have the ledgers shredded to confetti, and the computer disc could be anywhere. He only has to stamp on it, anything, and it's stuffed.'

Travis looked uncomfortable. 'And there's something else. It's what we didn't know about in the last raid. He works from a bunker beneath the house. Steel doors, grills, concrete . . .'

'There goes your two minutes,' Mickey said.

'That's all the time you've got.'

Ridgy stood up and walked over to where Travis was assembling his slides. He spoke quietly. 'I don't understand this way of doing things. You could easily grab him when he drives in after the races. Slap a search warrant on him and take him down to the bunker. You'd have his two sets of books and the computer disc.'

Travis looked up at Ridgy. 'What are you saying?'

'I'm saying,' Ridgy said, still in a whisper, 'that you're giving him a chance to destroy the evidence.'

'We do it this way. If we'd wanted your input on strategy we would've asked for it.'

'I think you've got a real police problem on your hands. If anyone is killed in this operation your mob will have to answer for this decision.'

Mickey watched the mansion flick up onto the screen. 'It's impossible,' he called out to Travis. 'It's a minute from the gate to the front door. And you're talking about heavy oxy and cutting work.'

'Sergeant McClintock, isn't it?' Travis said to Mickey.

'Yeah, that's right.'

'Well Sergeant, I'd suggest you shut up and start applying yourself . . . or maybe I ought to arrange for you to be absented from this operation.'

Ridgy put Travis straight. As a Rescue operation, they would be in charge until Travis's team were inside the bunker. Inspector Adams had sensed dispute and emerged from his glass bunker to enforce his authority. 'That's right, Travis,' he said. 'And if there's any absenting to be done, I'll be doing it.'

The questions for Travis ranged from Georgia's about the guard dogs, to Frog's query on the state-of-the-art monitoring gear. The dogs were to be taken care of with sedative darts. The cameras of the monitoring gear were to be taken care of by Rescue, and if there were guards, Special Operations would knock them down.

The meeting was cut short by an emergency call. An armed gunman had robbed a bank in one of the beach suburbs, Curl Curl. He had taken hostages, crashed a stolen car into an electricity pylon and then taken refuge in a nearby house.

Ridgy took command now.

He nominated Mickey and Georgia for his team.

Adams came out to inquire about Ridgy's health, but saw a different man. As the team ran to their vehicle, Adams called out. 'He's well-armed; he can use the weapon; he's doped up.'

'Aah,' Georgia commented on Adams's last words. 'How quaint. Doped up. A phrase from the seventies, I believe.'

'I wish we were back in the seventies,' Ridgy said. 'We'd probably know who were the good guys and who were the bad ones.'

'Yeah, on the Wilson thing?' Georgia said. 'I feel we're being led by the nose.'

'Why do you reckon?' Mickey asked as the vehicle slipped onto the coast road, its lights flashing; Ridgy judging distances beautifully through the traffic.

'Well,' Georgia said, 'first they reckon it's easy. And now he's in this impregnable bunker. Then he mentioned there were no guards, and now they reckon there might be.'

Ridgy slewed the wagon off the coast road. They saw the wreck immediately. It had blown apart in a profound way, and looked already as if it were trying to return to the soil. Ridgy was applying the brakes when the shots came. A high-pitched whine sounded several times from the motor as bullets hit it and spun off through the hood. The window shattered as Ridgy pulled the vehicle to the side of the road, and the three of them manoeuvred their way out of the passenger door. The red house from which the shots had been fired was high on the other side of the street, and their legs and feet would be protected by the body of the wagon.

Mickey sprinted for the wreck. 'Shit,' Ridgy said, as shots rang out. He saw the bloke was no marksman. He had no idea of leading his target with the sights in order to account for the speed of the runner. The bullets kicked up earth metres behind Mickey. He hadn't even cleared the venetian blinds in the windows for firing space.

Ridgy realised he could easily have taken this bastard if he'd had a rifle, but a faint nausea fluttered his stomach as he thought about doing it. No, there were other ways. But if Saturday was going to be a problem with him he'd better declare it as soon as he made it back.

Georgia had gone at a run to the neighbours out the other way, keeping the car between her and the gunman. She ran back to the wagon as Mickey was calling in from the wreck. 'We've got a woman here,' Mickey said. 'And she's pregnant.'

'God!' Georgia said. 'And he's got two young girls in the house.'

Ridgy stood, weighing the possibilities. Who was he going to need?

'I'll go to the woman,' Georgia said.

'Not through gunfire you won't,' Ridgy said. He called base for an ambulance and a doctor, telling them the story.

'What's her condition, Mickey?' he asked on the handset, his mind returning to the scene.

There was a delay while Mickey talked to the woman. 'Well, Ridgy, apart from being about to give birth, her legs are trapped beneath the seat. We're going to need the extractors. If it was a modern job I could've ripped the seats out myself.'

As Ridgy was calling base again, specifically to ask for an obstetrician, Georgia took the opportunity to dash for the wreck with the extractors. No shots followed her and that told Ridgy the bloke was sloppy, his heart wasn't in this conflict—and it hadn't even begun. The problem with a bloke like this, though, was he would be unpredictable. You could be lulled into carelessness because he wasn't firing. But the drug haze had only to lift and he'd be at the window again. And if he had uppers on him, all hell could break loose.

Ridgy called base. 'Have you got the phone number of this bloody house yet? You've had the address for about twenty minutes.'

Ridgy was alone with the decisions running through his mind. He opened the vehicle door and sat down on the running board. He could do nothing more until the Special Operations team arrived. The firearms they had aboard were hopeless for any kind of sniping shots, and anyway, there was no way he would endanger the kids in the house even if he had a powerful hunting rifle.

The thing that was really troubling him was the woman in the car. What if she suddenly decided the baby was due? He knew modern theory held that it was the baby who decided the time of its birth. He hoped the little bugger knew better than to choose this moment.

He stood up and watched Mickey and Georgia trying to place the extractors. Luckily the bloke hadn't been moved to fire on them. Any sort of high-powered bullet would have punctured the steel skin of the car.

For a moment the drama of the scene struck him. It became more than just a job of work. The human elements were suddenly very poignant. Apart from his two heroes, there were two terrified children in the house, a pregnant woman, and all their lives being ruled by a crazy with a rifle. He wondered how they were all enjoying their parts. Of course, it was Gina who had opened up for him the idea of the performer's needs. That was why he was now seeing the theatre of these bizarre circumstances. 'There's nothing in the world like when I'm on stage, I belong there,' she'd said. 'It's me. I need that.' How many actors did he have on his hands here? What part was the crazy playing? He could be desperately proud and certainly not prepared to relinquish his position if it would appear to be humiliating. At least Mickey and Georgia knew their parts.

Gina certainly knew hers. For a moment he resisted thinking about her. Get control of what's happening in front of you, he told himself. But there was nothing he could really do here for the moment but watch. He sneaked a look at his handgun, checked its load. Not that it would be worth anything in these conditions. Neither would the shotgun tucked beneath the shelf with the ropes. He simply couldn't keep his mind from the events of last night. He hadn't realised how much he could enjoy seeing a woman on display. And it was her obvious enjoyment of it that allowed him to acknowledge his liking for it. He had been completely tantalised as she removed her clothes in his bedroom. There was an element of mockery in her display, she was posing, making cute magazine movements as if they were something she wanted to turn into fun. He had been captivated. He laughed at himself. Next stop lingerie fetishest, he told himself. And what was he doing with thoughts of her now? If I try and reconnoitre at the back of the house I lose control of the action in front. I have to wait for back up.

Inside the living room of the red house the two girls were kneeling on the floor, their faces down on an old vinyl sofa. Julie tried to look at Wanda without moving her head. The last time she had moved a fraction she had been cuffed on the neck. She wanted to see if Wanda was all right. She seemed to be snuffling at the back of her throat, but maybe she was just crying. She guessed she hadn't been really hurt when they had been pushed to the floor. She hadn't cried out when the man had picked them up and dumped them in their present position.

Julie had been riding on her bike when the car had come careening around the corner out of control. She had jumped from her bike to get out of the way more quickly, but the car had slewed into the pylon before it reached her. The driver seemed to emerge from the car even before it was properly stopped, and had run for her. She had thought he wanted help and just stayed there. But there was a gun in his hand and he had grabbed her by the arm, and dragged her across to where her sister, Wanda, was standing stunned, her mouth open.

With his gun clasped under his arm, he had pushed them to the side of the car. He pulled open the back door and she had seen the woman. She was pregnant and her legs appeared to be stuck under the front seat. Her eyes pleaded to be left. 'Sorry about your car,' the man said, as if he were trying to make a joke, but his voice was shaky. He could see the woman would be too much trouble, and had dragged the two girls up to the house. The back door was unlocked. He pushed the girls in ahead of him, yelling out to any occupant, but the house was empty. Inside, he walked round locking the doors and windows.

Julie could see the madman had no idea what to do. He was like a school teacher dropped into a roomful of kids he's never taught before, and for the first half of a lesson tries to find out the structure of the class. Who were the boss kids, who were the workers, who were the smart-arses? Stuff like that.

But this teacher could not only clip their ears, keep them in after school, forbid them food or drink—he had a machine gun or something to back up his demands.

She saw Wanda had wet herself when the man began firing out the window. The noise had a frightening inevitability about it that was really depressing her.

'Can I have a drink of water?' she asked, to impose herself on the situation. She felt there had to be something between them and the man otherwise he wouldn't care about them at all. At the moment she didn't think he would care whether he shot them or not. He didn't answer for a while.

Then the man turned. She could hear the venetian blinds clicking back into place as he stopped looking through them.

'Shut up,' the man suddenly yelled. It was strange he had allowed so much time to pass before answering.

He walked over and grabbed her by the back of her dress, hauling her to her feet. Pushing her to the windows he made a gap in the blind and held her against the glass. Outside she saw the broken car, and then further up the hill a police truck with the circling blue lights. She thought if she were the man she'd shoot the lights out. 'Why don't you shoot the lights out,' she said. The man started laughing. It was an awful sort of laugh, as if there was nothing else left in him but that sound.

Then the man began to talk to them as if they were people again. 'Listen,' he said. 'I want you to stay on that couch and I don't want you talkin', right? If you want to go out the back you ask me. I'm gonna look afta' ya because they won't shoot at me if yous are here, right?'

Julie looked across at Wanda and saw she was getting herself together a bit. 'We're just real scared,' Julie said. 'You know, we don't want to muck around or anything.'

The man nodded, and she saw that he was really sweating, and the pulse in his neck was jumping around. She wondered why he was always running his hand through his hair. He jumped when a siren sliced through the air for a few seconds and then stopped.

★　★　★

Mickey looked at Susan Russell lying on the back seat. She seemed to have moved. Yeah, it was her stomach that was moving. He looked at her face. She was holding down the pain. There was a grimace fixed there. Don't let the baby come now, he told her silently. We can't even spread your legs yet. Georgia was fixing the extender clamps to either side of the car. To move the seat away from her legs they had to straighten the body of the car first.

'How are your legs?' he asked her.

'I don't really know what's happened to them,' she said.

'You'd know if they were broken,' Mickey said, but then he remembered that a woman about to give birth produced a natural pain-killer, not that it was ever much good judging by the screams he heard in the casualty wards when a soon-to-be-mother was rushed in.

'I can really feel him now,' Susan said to Mickey. 'He really wants to be born. I've been having contractions for a while I think. I couldn't really tell because of the pain in my legs, but that's going now.'

Mickey heard Ridgy's voice on the bull horn then.

'John,' Ridgy said, his voice echoing from the houses and nearby cliffs, 'I'm Peter Ridgeway from Police Rescue. I'd like to have a talk with you, John. Nice and easy. So, if you'd just answer the phone . . .'

Terrific, Mickey thought, they know his name now. We're getting somewhere.

Ridgy heard the phone lifted. John Down's voice was tight and edgy. It was sliding across contained fright. This bastard *was* dangerous: unpredictable. 'I got nothing to say. I'm not comin' out.'

That's great, Ridgy told himself. He's scared so shitless he can't even think. That meant he would either knuckle under when the pressure was applied, or go completely bloody crazy.

'John,' Ridgy continued, 'we've got a woman trapped in the car, and she's giving birth. If we don't get her out, both she and the baby could die. What I would like is for you to come out, and then everything can be organised safely. We're not going to hurt anyone.'

'Do you think I'm fuckin' mad,' Downs said. There was a pause and one of the girls came on the phone. 'Please,' Julie said, 'he said he'd hurt us. Come and help us, please.' The voice ended in a throaty gagging sound.

'Listen, copper bastards, you come near me and you're dead.' The voice had grown more confident as Downs remembered his hatred. Then the line went dead. The bastard must have ripped it out.

Ridgy called Mickey. 'Listen, Mick, there's no cease-fire. I wouldn't trust him even if he offered one anyway.'

'I hear you, Ridgy. Where's the doc?'

'Any time, now.'

Ridgy turned at the sound of a siren. He groaned at the sight of the Special Operations van. It pulled up behind him and disgorged its contents. The dozen men, dripping with weaponry, formed up along the side of the van away from the house.

The shots that rang up from the house hit the van and whined away over the ocean. The sounds seemed to Ridgy a sad protest. Poor Downs, poor kids. Downs had no idea of the fire power that could be poured into the red house.

Ridgy heard an old cohort, Sergeant Williams, direct the men to cover every aspect of the house. Williams approached Ridgy as soon as he saw all his men in place.

'G'day Ridgy,' Williams said. 'What have we got here?'

'He's ripped the line out so we can't talk him through all his little problems,' Ridgy said.

'Or magnify his fears, eh, mate?'

Ridgy nodded. 'That's about it.'

'So, we've got a cowboy with a death wish, eh?'

'You've got to take this really carefully. He'll kill those kids. He's strung out and wants power at any price.'

'Yeah, don't worry, Ridgy, we know this little bastard.' Williams took the bull horn from Ridgy and aimed it at the house. 'Special Operations team. Remember us, John? Yeah, I bet you do. I want you to put your rifle down and come out with your hands up.

'Do as I say and I promise no harm'll come to you. Now you don't want to make things worse for yourself, John. You don't want to hurt innocent people.'

Ridgy saw Georgia and Mickey begin cranking the extenders. He hoped the wreck wouldn't make any sudden noise as it underwent further structural change. Any unusual sound could begin a fire-fight, panic one of the cops close to the house, panic the kids, Downs, anyone. This was the moment an operation like this took its own path.

Williams continued. 'Just throw your rifle out the window and everything'll be OK.'

Up in the house they saw the venetian blinds pulled open and Downs again pressed a child to the window. 'Any of you copper bastards come up here and we all go.'

Mickey heard the desperate voice as he worked on the wreck, and felt horribly inadequate. Susan was having strong labour pains, her waters had broken, and the extenders were not going to free her. They would have if the floor hadn't been rusted out. He knew if they kept on cranking the vehicle would eventually collapse in further and it was a toss up whether the seat would spring upwards, or downwards, pinning her legs even tighter.

Susan saw that Mickey and Georgia were becoming very intent, gone was their earlier banter. 'It's not going to work is it?' she asked them.

'It sure is,' Mickey reassured her in a jovial tone. 'It won't be long now.' For one mad moment he thought if the baby started coming he might have to place the extenders between her knees to give the child room to be born.

He saw it for what it was, a mad solution thrown up in reaction to his state of near panic. What the hell were they going to do if the baby faced death between birth contractions and a non-existent exit? Even if the bastard in the house gave up now it wouldn't help them much.

'God, I'm thirsty,' Susan said. Mickey looked down at her. He had stopped winching the extender, and was pretending to do things while he worked out a strategy. He was wondering if he could force his own legs beneath the seat next to Susan's and force it up a little while her's were dragged out. It would be a really long shot. He was becoming attached to this woman. She knew her position, she hadn't panicked, and she was not putting any pressure on him or Georgia. He stopped a resigned shake of his head because it would have been a giveaway that things weren't progressing too well. He was certainly becoming involved with all the victims he was attending lately. He used to be able to breeze through rescues, enjoying his skills, giving the trapped and injured glib assurances and friendliness, without a thought.

He looked sideways at Georgia. Georgia was getting worried too. She held up a bottle of soft drink. 'Look what I've found, Susan. It was behind the seat.' She handed it to Susan. Mickey saw how grateful she was for that.

Mickey called Ridgy on his hand set. 'Hey mate, I need some cutters, can you get them to me?'

'Okay, Mickey.' Ridgy's voice sounded like clear support to Mickey. He knew they'd be on their way. He thought again of just standing up in the front of the car and heaving against the seat. The problem with that great idea was he would be an amazingly easy target for shithead in the house.

Williams explained a new problem to Ridgy. 'There is no way we can get any cover for our blokes facing the front of the house. No-one has a front garden in this street. On a roof they'd be silhouetted against the sea and be a cinch of a shot for him. No-one along here even has a chimney.' He wanted Ridgy to take a rifle on his run for it. 'You'd get a clear shot from behind the car. One of our blokes would scare the woman. And then the moment he puts his dial through the blinds, BAM. You'd blow his kisser off easy. You wouldn't even touch the kids. A clean head shot.'

'No, thanks. I can't do it any more. If I missed it would draw fire on the pregnant woman. Great.'

'You wouldn't miss, though, mate. You were the best we had.' Williams followed Ridgy to the back of the van where the cutters were clipped just inside the door. 'Ridgy, I remember the night you shot the bloke. We were all scared.'

'Yeah, but I pulled the trigger.'

'If it had been me, mate, I would have shot too. So would any of us.'

'And whoever it was would feel like I do right now.'

Williams grabbed his arm as he was about to head off. 'Those people down there, they're your friends, and you've got a kid about to be born. They're

37

depending on you. This is what we've been trained for, mate.'

Ridgy knew Williams was casting around desperately for something that would motivate him, and this appeal found its mark, no matter that Williams didn't genuinely feel it. He looked down at Williams and then headed back to the armourer at the rear of the Special Operations vehicle. 'Give us a rifle.'

Along with the rifle Ridgy was handed a bullet-proof vest. Mickey's voice came over the handset. 'Ridgy, mate. Ridgy, I need to talk to a doctor right now. Get one patched through.'

Ridgy heard the sound of the helicopter as he prepared to make a run for it. 'Listen, Mickey,' he called. 'The doc is in the chopper. And I'm on my way.'

*   *   *

The three in the front room of the house raised their heads as they heard the helicopter. Downs kicked at the table and hurt his foot. He hopped around the room. Wanda laughed, an hysterical giggle, and he charged across the room and whacked her across the face. 'You little bastards ... one word, one fuckin' word, right?' He held the gun up. Julie noticed he didn't actually point it at either of them. She saw also that Wanda's tears alarmed him. He wanted to do something to make them stop.

The thought forming in Julie's mind was that Downs wanted somebody else to take control. She knew a twelve year old wasn't expected to know this sort of thing, but she saw that when the helicopter was approaching, it all seemed too much for him. He kept putting the gun down and picking it up again. He looked out the window, and suddenly threw it open and fired wildly. Julie had no idea what was going on. He didn't really seem to be aiming at anything. If he was he would have hit somebody she thought. The car wasn't much more than the length of a basketball court away.

'I reckon they'd let you go,' she said.

'Shut up,' he said. 'They don't let you go, not those bastards. They'll kill me.'

'You could ask them,' she said.

'They're lyin' bastards,' he said, as he looked out the window again.

★　★　★

The moment Ridgy saw Downs turn away he ran for it. It would take Downs at least three seconds to turn again, clear the blinds, aim and fire. He could get at least thirty metres in that time. Those seconds passed in slow motion. He felt really vulnerable out there, trying to pump his legs faster. His speed seemed non-existent, as in a dream. He made it though, and slid in behind the wreck, coming to a stop next to Georgia. Several shots slammed into the roof of the wreck. 'His timing's off,' Georgia said, looking at Susan. 'Don't worry, love, he doesn't want to hurt us.' Ridgy and Mickey looked at each other.

Mickey looked at the rifle. 'You think you'll nail him if he runs down here?'

'He won't,' Ridgy answered. 'The doctor might need some help getting down here, though.'

'They won't let the doctor come,' Mickey said.

'And what we have here is a seat that can't be moved with a short jemmy. But the rifle might be just the thing.'

Ridgy uncoupled the magazine from the rifle and snapped the cartridge out of the breech. He handed Mickey the rifle with the breech open.

'I know it's ridiculous,' Mickey said. 'But couldn't Special Ops trundle their van down here and hide us from the house?'

'They'll never do it. It puts the driver at risk, and the van is a priority. It's not to be damaged.'

'What about the bloody priority here?' Mickey said, as he moved out of the front door, stepped between Georgia and Ridgy, and slipped the butt of the rifle under the seat. He applied a little pressure on the rifle jemmy and thought he could get considerable purchase.

'Georgia,' Mickey said. 'I want you to move around me so you can help Susan shift her legs.'

His handset crackled to life as he was about to apply his strength. It was the doctor.

'I'm Louise Hardy,' the doctor said. 'Is the patient in shock?'

Mickey motioned to Georgia to take the handset. Georgia swung away to one side, her back to the rear tyre. Ridgy took her place.

'Susan, the patient, is very calm, doctor,' Georgia said.

'Was she hurt in the accident?'

'A small scalp wound. We don't know about her legs, they're still stuck, but there doesn't appear to be too much pain. Our problem is the baby. Her membrane's broken and she's having contractions.'

40

'How far apart?'

'Two minutes.'

Mickey braced himself and heaved. A bolt snapped somewhere, and he redoubled his strength to keep the pressure on. To let the seat down on the legs now would be unthinkable. Criminal. His strength was still in his legs, so he continued increasing pressure there, easing up on his arms, waiting until he felt the weakness in his legs before he used his arms again.

'When's the baby due?' Mickey heard the doctor ask.

'Two weeks,' Georgia answered.

'Is Susan able to bend her knees?'

'Negative,' Georgia said.

'Can you move her legs apart?'

'About six inches,' Georgia said. 'Six inches at the knee that is.'

Mickey gave one last heave. Bolts pulled from the steel and the seat moved. 'Jesus, get her out, Ridgy. I can't hold it much longer.' He could feel a definite force that was preventing him moving it any further. It must have been the way the seat crumpled, making the steel stronger than it would normally have been.

Ridgy moved Susan's legs out, and tears flooded her eyes. The relief brought joy. Mickey let the seat go as gently as he could. There was a loud cracking sound as the steel took its original position.

The sound was loud enough to be heard in the house. Downs ran to the window and peered through the slats. He couldn't identify where the sound had come from, and it made him edgy. 'I need a drink,' he said to Julie, without looking at her.

'I'll look in the cupboards,' she suggested. He nodded.

She walked to the cupboard, looking at him, not where she was going. 'Watch out,' he said. In one cupboard she found glasses, and in another, some whisky and gin. She poured a whisky, half a glass.

'Thanks,' Downs said, still looking out.

Ridgy was surprised to see Downs at the venetians. He had pushed the magazine home again, and was letting the bolt slide home with a round in the breech when the head disappeared. I wouldn't have done it anyway, he told himself.

When Downs turned around the two girls were whispering by the cupboard. 'I need to go to the toilet,' Wanda said.

Downs sipped the drink. 'No, wait, sit down.'

'It's all right. Let her go.'

Julie knew the absolute rightness of her next move. She pushed Wanda towards the hall door, and threw herself at Downs. 'Run, run,' Julie yelled at Wanda as she found herself holding onto Downs by the arm. She lifted her feet off the ground in pure reflex to give herself more weight. He shook her off pretty easily, but by that time Wanda had gone. Julie could hear her fumbling with the front door but then it slammed almost instantly. Downs kept pointing the rifle at her as he ran for the window. She calculated she could escape the same way if he didn't turn from the window, but as he peeped through the blind, he was still holding the muzzle of the weapon steady on her.

And then Downs was firing through the window. Julie was stunned. Wanda was being shot. It was her fault. She ran for him again.

Outside, Mickey had heard the scream, realised Georgia could cope now, that he would only be in the way, and had begun moving towards the house. The bastard would be occupied by whoever was doing the screaming. He wouldn't be watching from the window. And then the front door burst open and a young girl ran from the house. He was twenty metres from her and she ran straight towards him rather than to the safety of the side of the house. Mickey realised it would have been better if he hadn't been there.

He quickly grabbed her and made for the side of the house in a dead run. He saw Downs at the window, heard the crack of the rifle and saw another girl throw herself at Downs. He didn't think he'd been hit. Even as he ran he was checking the remoter parts of his body for pain or the disappearance of feeling. Nothing. The bastard had been shooting up the car again. Most of the bullets he had fired he had placed in the engine hood. Away from Downs's view Mickey rested with the girl. He was safe here, there were no windows overlooking them.

Looking down at the wreck he saw Ridgy with his rifle moving beneath the underside of the boot. He was brave, the petrol tank was above him. Downs would be surprised. He wouldn't be expecting a bullet from that direction. 'Shoot him, Ridgy,' Mickey yelled. 'Take the bastard out.'

Ridgy caught Downs's face in the telescopic sight, the crossed hairs on the lens neatly dissecting his forehead. He could have pulled the trigger then. No-one would have complained, even questioned him about it. If he were a killer he certainly would have done it. But he was relying on instinct now. This bloke wasn't about to hurt anyone. And Ridgy knew he wouldn't be able to go on living with two questionable homicides to his name. He'd wait until a different sort of shot presented itself. A high-powered two-fifty such as he had could change the hydraulics of the human body, wound and place a man instantly into shock. He wasn't going to kill.

Julie watched Downs. He had pushed her roughly back to the sofa, but he hadn't used any real strength. She began to feel that her only danger now might be from the police firing into the house and killing her accidentally.

But she was unprepared for the impact on Downs when it came. The blinds, the window, and Downs seemed to explode. He was thrown across the room, his shoulder sprung with shattered bone like the spines of an angry anteater. The sound deafened her, but she knew it was time to run.

Out at the wreck Ridgy yelled, 'Got him.' He called out to the ambulance crew. 'Get him out of there. He'll be bleeding.'

The Special Operations blokes went in hard, still wary of a response from Downs. Ridgy went up to the ambulance officers. 'Follow them up. He won't be feeling like doing anything, if he's feeling anything at all, but watch them.' The ambulance drivers ran with a stretcher. They called out they were coming some metres from the house. This was for two reasons. They didn't want to be shot, and it was also a warning to the Special Operations blokes to stop working over their victim. They had been on such jobs before, and had once seen them bashing the culprit like greyhounds savaging a rabbit skin on a lure.

Mickey walked down to Ridgy with Wanda. The kid was quivering.

'Great shot, Ridgy,' Mickey said. He didn't know why he felt so relieved. But he remembered then the raid they would be making on Saturday after the races. It would be good to know that Ridgy was so capable of backing-up. Ridgy had been through the fire. He was no longer a trigger-happy dipstick. He knew when things were hazardous enough to warrant a violent response.

Williams came up to Ridgy, smiling. Mickey left to see how Susan was holding up. Georgia had it all in hand. Susan was on a stretcher and another ambulance crew were preparing to load her aboard.

'How're ya going?' Mickey asked her.

'I think this baby's going to arrive before I make it to hospital,' Susan said. 'I don't care though, after what I've gone through it can only get better.' Mickey followed her to the ambulance. He picked up her hand and squeezed it. She squeezed back, hard. 'I was scared,' she said gravely, flashing back to how it had been. 'But I just knew you wouldn't let anything happen to me.'

Mickey was staggered. There was some truth in that, he knew. Her instinct was good. He just didn't want to be bound by such an image of himself—it was too scary, too much responsibility. Would he *always* place himself in danger if challenged? It was something he might have to change. Although maybe then he wouldn't inspire such confidence in people. But then, his confidence also came from Rescue back-up. Today, too, it had come from knowing the woman had great reserves of strength. Her showing that had stopped him going into a fluster mode, something he often did around women in danger.

The ambulance with Downs left with the siren piercing the sultry afternoon air. Susan grimaced. Mickey smiled at her as she was lifted into the ambulance.

He began packing his gear when a scream he was familiar with rent the air. The baby was close. He turned his head to look at the ambulance. For the moment it wasn't going anywhere. God, it had been close. He and Georgia attempting to manipulate the baby would have been a disaster. Ridgy was walking alongside the ambulance and stopped suddenly. Mickey heard it too. The baby was crying. One of the ambulance crew opened the door and came out grinning. 'No problems,' he said. Susan's ambulance moved gently away, only the lights flickering.

Four

Ridgy drove back with Georgia and Mickey. He hardly said anything. He could imagine how the other two were feeling. They had the calm of knowing they had performed satisfactorily. Mickey had been pretty high immediately after the action, but now he settled into feeling good about being alive. Georgia was wondering how she would have stood up to having a baby in those conditions. She knew she wouldn't have had *one* vital aspect required for surviving the ordeal—faith in the police force. Sure, there were certain miracles they could perform, but a madman with a gun could never be discounted, no matter how many police surrounded you.

Ridgy was anxious to see Gina. He felt a definite need for her companionship, her presence; there was a feeling he deserved her now. He had faced the fire and won through. He had left Special Operations with terrible questions about himself. For a fraction of a moment before he had pulled the trigger on that terrible day so long ago he had felt the satisfaction of using the weapon for which he had been trained. Whether the pleasure had been that he was about to kill with it, had been something else. The emotions of the day had been somewhat buried under the devastation of learning he had killed an innocent person, that the man had a wife and three children. That the kids would be looking for their father to come home for a good part of their lives.

Whatever it had been so long ago, he had survived it, had moved through that desire to kill. He had held his fire when he had the perfect target for a kill. He had rid himself of immature heroics. He knew how he could do a job differently, successfully, and he had done it his way. It somehow expunged the guilt of being the trigger-happy loon that he had been trained to be. How did that free him to love Gina more? He had no idea, but there was certainly a removal, or loosening, of self-imposed bonds.

'I'm going to ring the hospital when we get back,' Georgia said.

Mickey leaned forward to look at her. 'You're feeling it too,' he accused.

'What are you talking about?'

'You feel involved with these people we save every day.'

'Of course I do. You mean you haven't been?'

'It's happening more and more,' he answered. He sank back against the seat. 'We shouldn't be,' he said.

'Bullshit,' Georgia said. 'You don't believe all that muck you get in training, do you? They just want to keep us from getting involved in real problems because they think we wouldn't be on call to work at everything they throw at us. Then they'd have to spend more money.'

Ridgy laughed. 'She's right, Mickey. They want us to be automatons. Do this. Do it this way. Stop. Do this over there. Be objective.'

'Yeah,' Georgia said. 'Only they don't mean objective. They mean think like us. Make everything look good as quickly as possible.'

Mickey began humming to himself, but Georgia heard and she looked at him curiously. What she and Ridgy had described was exactly what Mickey had liked about the job. Everything was over at the end of the day's work. You didn't carry burdens around with you. You were ready and eager do their bidding again first thing next day.

Georgia followed up her point. 'And they don't want you to pass on your experience to people you've helped,' she said. 'They don't even want you to learn. They want reliable machines.'

Mickey saw how wrong he had been for a long time. He had felt the uneasiness growing on him. For weeks now he had been feeling as if he were being used, as if Adams was getting at him. Now, he knew, it wasn't even Adams, it was those big wigs who didn't understand that the coppers who did the dirty work were human as well. Or perhaps they understood all right, but didn't care.

'You were good with Susan,' Georgia said to Mickey. 'Really gentle.'

'Yeah, well, I'm a pretty good actor.'

'Sure. But not today you weren't. That wasn't acting.'

'No . . .' he said thoughtfully.

Ridgy listened to Georgia. She was a really smart young woman and she probably had clues that would help him in his relationship with Gina. He had heard about the new consciousness sweeping the world. It wasn't new at all. Communities had always cared about their people. Coppers had walked the beat for years being part of the community, but now they were removed from it all by skills and technology. Not that there hadn't been terrible problems in the force, brutality and corruption. Now, though, there was a pride in being hard-boiled, caring for nothing but the skills of the job. He knew where Mickey was coming from all right. Perhaps it was going to change again, with people like Mickey coming to realise how things really were. As for himself, Gina had already dramatically changed him. He had been developing a self-pitying bitterness, and the demands of his job had hidden it from him. With his awareness of her had come a new look at himself.

Gina had shown him another side to life too, one he had never really known about. Some people loved their jobs with an intensity that bordered on obsession. Her singing wasn't really a job. It was a love. Last night she had told him, 'I couldn't live if I couldn't perform. It's as if I'm helping people understand something. I'm giving them something to think about. You know what I mean, don't you?' He hadn't, because he had assumed she was only trying to create lust, but it slowly dawned on him that if he could understand that as theatre, it would be helpful.

'You mean they're understanding the emotions in the music?' he had asked her.

'That's what I mean, the music. It's inside you. You can feel it moving you, making things happen.'

Ridgy hadn't agreed with that, but he hadn't said anything. It was a bit like needing a crutch in order to live. Like someone having faith in God, and without that faith being unable to face their day. Not that that wasn't better than the nothing some people had to cope with. He supposed it meant that Gina could cope very well without him. Why couldn't he accept that? He knew he would have to.

Then she had asked him, 'What do *you* really want?'

'You for starters,' he'd said.

'Mmm,' she said. 'But I mean your work. What does it give you? You like it don't you?'

'Right at this very moment I couldn't care less about it. I could walk away right now. Could you walk away from your music?'

'No,' she said. 'I never would.'

Later he realised that at the time they were talking he hadn't understood what was really going on. She had been telling him he could never be as important to her as her music, and he had been saying she was everything to him. It niggled him a bit. He thought it might change, but then he saw she had already had the best of him. There wasn't too much more, and he hadn't put a dent in her career ambitions.

Hey, he tried to tell himself, that's fine. That's how it should be. He had read that's how it should be, and he would agree that it was right, but somehow, now it was part of a relationship of his, he wasn't so sure.

At the depot Mickey and Georgia checked the gear as he went to put in the paperwork. They seemed to be working very perfunctorily, although quickly, and it was something he noted, but forgot about until he saw them leave together, each in their own car, at the same speed, and Mickey taking Georgia's direction, rather than turning south to his place.

So Gina and I aren't the only ones around here. Ridgy laughed at himself. For a split second he had felt indignant that the two of them were breaking the unwritten rule of no romantic attachments in the work place.

*   *   *

Georgia's unit looked over Pittwater, a marvellous stretch of water for boating, fishing, feeding the kids to sharks—which patrolled the sandbanks after the shoals of fish that came to feed on the inlet debris— and for simple and satisfying contemplation.

Georgia and Mickey weren't doing much contemplating though, intent as they were on getting each other out of their clothes as quickly as possible. On such a warm evening clothes seemed superfluous to the activity they were quickly getting down to. The French windows were open to the view, and the breeze coming in from the ocean caressed their bodies as warmly and lightly as the caresses they gave each other. Sydney was becoming the financial capital of Australia, perhaps for the very reason that this sort of open air activity could be indulged freely here for nine months of the year. In Melbourne it was pretty much restricted to a short summer of ten weeks—in a good year!

At the very moment they were moaning their appreciation of each other's lovemaking, a huge rig with twin Volvo diesels was making its way into the bay loaded with twenty kilos of high grade coke from South America. Of course the rig hadn't made the ocean crossing, it had simply picked up a package thrown from a cargo vessel just out of the bay. On the bridge were several big men, laughing and drinking beer from cans. Vic Wilson was one of them. He was being cut into the big money so that the drug syndicate that some of Sydney's bigger developers were involved in, could control his laundering operation. Wilson knew that if he hadn't agreed to the arrangement he would have been lost forever in the vast ocean edging the city.

If Mickey had picked up Georgia's binoculars he might have recognised Wilson on the flybridge. What would he have thought? What could he have done? Nothing. The big crime lords of the city were protected by a police system controlled by an intricate system of political favours. Money in the hands of developers could buy anything, including the disappearance of trouble-makers. One person, who had attempted to save some of the best parts of Sydney for the people who had lived there all their lives, had been killed. Newspapers had destroyed the results of their reporters' investigations into that affair. Sydney was a closed city. It tarted itself up with cultural events and happenings to distract its intelligentsia. Hey, we're having fun! Let's not look at the real business of this great metropolis—crime!

By the time Mickey and Georgia walked out onto the balcony with their drinks the big rig had berthed at the marina wharf, and the coke was in a van travelling to a warehouse in the western suburbs. Vic Wilson was already driving home to his mansion. He had been really impressed by the operation. He had chosen to take part in it because he was putting his money in. He was glad he had. It was so simple as to be stunningly beautiful. A crew member dumped a package over the side of the ship as the garbage and bilge water was being released before it entered the harbour.

The twenty-five metre rig had travelled at right-angles across the ship's line. The sound system on the rig boomed out music from Vangelis, and young women walked the deck sipping drinks. To an on-looker it was the wealthy at play.

Built into the bow with the sonar gear was a sound detector attuned to the sealed battery device attached to the floating drug cache. The battery gave no clue as to its contents, Vic saw later. It was heavily coated in strong, moulded grey plastic, with a metal handle shaped like a horseshoe protruding from the top. It was by this it was attached to the package.

The drug cache itself was packed water-proof and weighted to float just below the surface. As the rig approached for the pick-up the women were guided to the entertainment cabin for more drinks. Up in the bow cockpit a scuba diver waited in case they were unable to locate and lift the treasure. The pick-up had gone smoothly though. And on the way back into the harbour Vic had been entertained by a very pretty young woman who kept asking him if he were a builder.

Such are the spoils of crime. The young woman felt depressed after the effort, but her carpenter husband was out of work, and she was doing what she could: 'Aah, yeah, there might be a chance to get your husband some work. Never know who you'll meet on the boat.' Well, she'd met Vic, but Vic wasn't about to give her husband anything. He just thought she'd be a grouse sheila to show around at the restaurants and clubs he ate at every night. Vic needed glamour and movement because he couldn't stand his own company for more than a few minutes at a time.

* * *

Mickey agreed with Georgia that Saturday's raid was suspect. 'It might be just a show raid,' Mickey said. 'Hell, you know that no-one could expect us to get anywhere in three minutes or whatever. A bloody concrete compound under the house? You've got to be bloody joking.'

'What does anyone gain?' Georgia asked.

'I dunno,' Mickey said. 'Maybe it'll look good on the media. Maybe they're trying to stop an inquiry or something. You know, they'll pull any stunt to stop people feeling they have to ask questions.'

Meanwhile, Ridgy was battling an approaching dread. He could feel it out there somewhere, he just had no idea from which direction it was going to clout him.

He had to admit that a relationship with Gina didn't feel real to him. She had chosen him on some whim probably. And yet, wasn't that how some relationships took off? But she was beautiful; he was ordinary. He felt if he didn't find out what his attraction was to her he wouldn't be able to capitalise on it, develop it, use it even. He'd forgotten the words he'd told Mickey: 'The technique is that there is no technique.'

On the other hand he concluded the dread may have nothing to do with Gina. Saturday's raid wasn't exactly going to be a piece of cake. Special Operations were going in on the slender possibility that they could snatch evidence that could easily be flushed, hidden, shredded, or stuffed up a large dog's arse. There were two large dogs and they sure wouldn't sit still for probing. Even the plan to disable them with darts was dicey. A dart gun was, by definition, inaccurate. You'd have to get within twenty metres of them to be sure of accuracy. Rousing them to come to the fence and within range would set them barking. That small element could jeopardise the whole raid. There were too many unknowns.

When Gina arrived at his house the feeling of dread disappeared immediately.

She had no hesitation in hugging him, responding to his lips and tongue, following him to the bedroom. As a kid he had often gazed at the underwear and corset advertisements in the *Women's Weekly* and wondered whether he would ever get to see the real thing on a real woman. He never had really. Ridgy had married a woman who was ashamed of her body and of his, and so his childhood fantasies were still pretty well intact. Well, they were more than fulfilled by the gear Gina wore. It was slithery and fetching, and slipped effortlessly from the body.

In fact it was too much for him.

It was all there waiting for him, but the Gina he thought he knew had disappeared somehow. He was unsure of what had happened. She was too pliant and receptive, and he couldn't understand this sea change, for he had barely touched her. She was away with her lust without his help. Far ahead of him. It was as if he were no longer present. He suspected he was being used, in some obscure fashion, as an object. Gina must have understood this somehow, because she became more focused on him and he relaxed and responded.

Afterwards they had a pasta dinner and walked along the Bondi beachfront.

'There was some trouble today?' Gina broached the subject of the shooting.

'Yeah,' Ridgy said.

'You shot someone.'

'Yeah, but he was threatening a kid.' Ridgy was a little defensive.

Gina touched his arm. 'I know, I know, it's quite all right. I mean, you're a hero.'

'No,' he said. 'Just someone doing his bloody job.'

'But you didn't kill him. Everyone said most people would have.'

Ridgy had a sudden flash. Was she in love with the way he did his job? Or what he'd done? Had that been at the centre of her lovemaking? 'Do you like working with the squad?' he asked her.

'Yes, I do,' she answered. 'I've met you, haven't I?'

'But Adams is such a prick,' Ridgy said.

'He's no trouble. He's not a vicious man.'

'What do you mean?'

'Well some men try and use their position to impress upon young women the seriousness of their attentions. You know, things like that.'

'Like me, you mean?' Ridgy asked, smiling at her.

'I like to choose my men,' she said. The feeling of dread became a sharp blade, and Ridgy felt the thrust of jealousy close to his heart. What the hell did she mean by men?

He went to sleep that night thinking about the coming raid. He had most of the logistical stuff down pat, but he was anxious about what his people would find through the front door.

Five

'Bullet-proof vests,' Georgia said. 'Elegant aren't they?'

'You've got to be kidding. We're not wearing these are we?' Angel asked.

Georgia held the vest up at arms length. Somehow her life had changed and she had been unaware of the turning point. She could remember the loneliness of farm life, the feeling that nothing would ever happen to her of any significance: where was that feeling now? For years she had imagined it being the indelible emotion of her life. Well, it was gone now.

Angel dropped the vest on the table. It offended his clothing sense. Georgia grinned at him. Angel had beautifully styled hair; his Rescue gear always looked as if it had been tailored for him. She suspected Angel, or more probably his mother, did some rapid needle work. 'We've got to wear this stuff,' she said. 'Some Special Ops bloke dropped them in. He said it was compulsory for this sort of operation.'

Angel stopped at the door. 'I'd feel like Ned Kelly in that stuff.'

'Yeah,' Georgia said. 'And look what happened to him.'

'They hung him.'

'They shot him first.'

Angel picked up the jacket again, holding it by the shoulders. 'I couldn't work in this.'

'Regulations, mate,' Georgia said, hoisting hers over her shoulders and walking into the squad room for the final briefing before the raid. Angel followed her.

Ridgy waited for them to find seats, and then began his spiel. Sergeant Travis was there, tapping a wooden pointer in the palm of his hand. Ridgy borrowed the pointer and gestured at the screen.

'Right,' Ridgy said to Travis. 'One of your blokes takes out the dogs, then Rattray and McClintock will come over the western wall here, and gel the cameras . . . here and here.'

'Gel?' Travis asked.

'Yes,' Ridgy said, 'we put a gelled screen over the lens. It'll look like circuit failure.' Travis nodded.

'Right,' Ridgy continued. 'This is our only entrance to the house, the side gate. The front gate is in full view of the neighbours across the street. We might have to use the acetylene gear to cut through the lock, slower than a cutter but it's quiet. If we can do the job without being seen from the house, we go over the fence. That will be decided later.'

Mickey cut through Ridgy's detail with a question for Travis. 'This bunker you're talking about: is it steel on bricks? Do the windows, if there are any, have bars?'

'Yes to both questions,' Travis answered. 'Our informant hasn't been able to tell us where the barred windows are, but we suspect it may be a skylight in the courtyard of the house. Our informant has only overheard some talk in various nightclubs.'

Mickey began imposing himself on the briefing.

Ridgy might be senior sergeant, but Mickey felt he needed to assert his own significance on this job, because he would be leading the team in. They would have to be looking forward to him and not backwards to Ridgy, who would be dealing with communications.

'OK, Angel will be using the cutter when we get to the bunker. Makes a hell of a racket but Wilson'll know we're on him by then.' Mickey turned to Travis. 'You blokes come barrelling through the gates, through the house, and into the central courtyard, which is also the roof of the bunker. We get rid of the grill, and you drop down through the skylight.'

Travis raised his hand. 'Just one thing. How're you gonna get us through the main gates?'

'Well as I see it you'll go over the wall but if we need to get you through the main gates that's where Angel first comes in.' He gestured to Angel. 'He disables the alarm without breaking the circuit. He can do that in seconds.'

'I didn't know we had an alarm systems bloke in Rescue. Where did you get your training?'

Angel looked a trifle awkward. His history on the streets could place him under severe discrimination in the future if it was revealed. 'Well, um . . .'

'Adelaide,' Mickey answered for him.

'Yeah,' Angel said, Adelaide . . . Tech.'

From the briefing room the squad moved into the warehouse and workshop. It was here they had roughly laid out the mansion's safety barriers. The iron gates, the cameras, the grills. They had the use of the strongest materials so their timing of the torching and cutting would be overestimated. The first time around they were sluggish. Angel kept pushing at his jacket as it caught at him when he leaned into his work.

Travis was very critical of the time. 'Three minutes twenty seconds, and that's just for the work. We haven't taken into account the running about. Wilson's shredded his records and we've missed out on a conviction.'

Mickey shook his head. 'Listen, you're spending a lot of time and money on this operation, and it has about a five per cent chance of succeeding. That's just supposing that Wilson and his mates panic and try and eat the stuff instead of shredding it. You know the dangers of this job as well as we do. It will be your fault if this job doesn't work, because you haven't grabbed him and his books as he leaves the course, on his way home, or at the front gates. Do you understand what we think this is about?'

Travis looked hard at Mickey and walked to the door of the warehouse and looked out.

'OK fellas,' Ridgy said, 'we'll do it again, and we'll keep at it until we're down to two minutes.'

Travis walked back to observe the next exercise, but didn't take up Mickey's challenge.

'I can't move in this bloody thing,' Angel said.

'McClintock's men are bullet proof as well, hey?' Travis commented.

'You said there were no guards,' Mickey said. 'No, sorry, *you* were going to take care of them, that right?'

Travis turned away shaking his head. 'You bloody blokes have got no discipline and too much lip. We're done from the start.'

'Up yours,' Mickey commented.

The squad worked at the exercises until they were

down to two minutes ten on the manual work. It wasn't going to get any faster.

In the locker room Angel showered and changed before the others had shed the fatigue of the work. 'See you later, guys,' Angel called.

'I reckon we're being set up on this operation,' Frog said to Mickey and Ridgy. The accusation was like an official complaint. He wanted to be let into the real story.

Ridgy sat down to take his boots off. Mickey closed his locker door and leaned against it.

'We've all got our doubts,' Mickey said.

'We'll certainly have to cover our arses. Our reports are gonna have to be very highly detailed,' Ridgy commented.

'Yeah,' Frog said. 'So you blokes know something?'

'Nothing specific, Frog,' Ridgy said.

'Well, what do you both think?'

'We think,' Mickey said, looking at Ridgy, challenging him to deny it, 'that the raid is covering up something else. Either the lack of real activity, or some cop's involvement with Wilson.'

'If it's that well organised there shouldn't be any shooting at us then,' Frog said.

'This is all theory,' Ridgy said. 'But it's not a practical operation. I mean these blokes could fix their books in a car, a motel, even a quiet pub. Why are they so certain it's happening in a bunker? No-one would build a bunker just to fix his books. He'd travel around, be elusive, rather than put in something like that. A bunker you might use for a drug lab, but not at your own house. There's too many things that don't add up.'

'The bunker might be for him to live in if he wants to double-cross his mates. Maybe this stuff is even hotter than we think,' Mickey said.

Shoeless and sockless, Ridgy put his foot on the bench and wiggled his toes. He looked up at Frog. 'The raid might even be to get him in closer with new people. Convince them the operation he has is dangerous, and that they wouldn't want to take it off him. Which means,' Ridgy added, as he looked down at his toes, 'that someone in the force is really in this thing. That this is a political and commercial act we're on. I just hope it's not.'

'Hell,' Frog said, 'my old man was on the take for forty years, and he gets a CBE for it. This stuff goes on all the time. The big boys never get nobbled, they've got too much influence.'

'Anyone for a beer?' Mickey asked.

'No,' Frog said. 'I like it too much.'

'I was thinking of a quiet night,' Ridgy said.

'Yeah, you need one,' Mickey commented.

'Dinner, and a quiet night,' Ridgy emphasised.

'Running you ragged, is she mate?'

'Leave it, Mick.'

Frog wandered to the door yawning. 'Did you blokes know that Special Ops have lost three men on their last five outings?'

'That's all I need to know,' Mickey said.

*　*　*

Ridgy and Gina had a chocolate dinner before they hit the bed to get on with their physical indulgences. Ridgy had bought the chocolates on a whim and they ate them slowly as they talked. They decided on a restaurant, even the sort of restaurant—Thai—but then one embrace led to another and their combined lust carried them into the bedroom.

To Ridgy it seemed perfect, and then, being one of the old school sentimentalists, he spoiled it all.

Lying back, looking at the sun bursting through the foliage outside the bedroom window, he realised that his life at this very moment could not be better. If I died now, he thought, it would be with a smile on my face. As he hadn't had very many of these moments, he wasn't experienced enough to know that they are not to be entirely trusted. Getting off the bed he went to the wardrobe, pulled out a drawer, took the small package taped to the back of it and returned to the bed.

Gina was oblivious to all this. She was deep into the sleep of the well satisfied, and the moisture of exhaustion ran from her mouth.

She woke slowly. One eye fluttered, and from that she glimpsed something large and alien watching her from the pillow. The other eye sprang open. It was a necklace. It was old—very old. The silver had the fine work you rarely saw these days except in an antique object. It was contained in the dent of the pillow. She looked up quickly. Ridgy was smiling at her, looking rather silly.

He picked up the necklace and held it out to her.

'Oh Peter, it's beautiful,' she said.

'So are you,' said the dopey big bastard.

'This must have cost you a fortune,' she said. 'You shouldn't have.'

'Do you like it?' asked the beaming Ridgy.

'It's wonderful. I love it.'

'It's a family heirloom. It belonged to my father's mother.'

Gina saw many things sweeping before her eyes. They all carried heavy labels like responsibility, obligation—and closed doors.

'This was your grandmother's?'

Ridgy nodded: she must see how serious he was. She certainly did.

'Peter, I can't.'

'But I want you to have it.'

'Peter, it's not right—it's the timing or something.'

'The timing doesn't matter,' said Ridgy, who owed his life many times over to the right timing.

Gina shook her head. 'No, Peter.'

'But why? You love me don't you? I know I love you.'

'Yes I know you do. Look, I don't want to hurt you, but remember what I said about the music.'

'Hey,' Ridgy said, hearing an imploring note in his voice. 'I like you being in the band.'

'No, it's more than that. It's what I do. The music is my life. There is nothing else. You'd just end up getting hurt and, well, we're having fun aren't we?'

'Is that all it is? Fun?'

'Fun is very important to me. Not many people have any fun at all. You have to work at it.'

'Yeah, but it sort of indicates that the moment fun leaves off for a while, it will be all over.'

'Well this isn't fun; talking about it.' Damn, she thought, I didn't want this to happen.

Ridgy moved to the window. A few minutes ago he had been blissfully happy. Now the sun was a pain.

Coping with the glare was depressing.

'Hey, look at me,' she said. 'I'll resign from the squad on Monday. If we see each other again it might be fun. But no-one ever tries to control me. I can't live like that.'

She placed the necklace back on the pillow. The sun caught it instantly. Such beautiful work. Such a very tempting object. It was unfortunate for Ridgy that Gina could create her own form of beauty, for herself and lots of others, and on balance she loved her work more than that of others. Not that he would have wanted a woman who could be bought with little treasures.

Watching her dress quickly, the shape of her body began to swim. Christ, thought Ridgy, what a baby, and he forced back the burning wetness threatening his eyes.

'Why me?' he asked her as she reached the door.

'You're very strong,' she said. 'Your type doesn't play personal politics. You don't think you're God's gift to anyone, and you won't judge me. Not only that, I will always be glad to see you. I like you.'

*   *   *

Mickey left home very early on Saturday. He wanted to talk to Georgia before she left for the depot. He hadn't ever really wanted to do more in the way of police work than he was doing with Rescue, but now, feeling used, abused, he wanted to *know* a great deal bloody more. Rarely had he ever schemed. He was as open as he could be. His responses weren't planned; he didn't want to be caught up in deception in any way. One of his friends had told him he was honest because he was lazy. 'You just can't be bothered playing the career game because you don't want to work at not being caught out.' He had thought that was pretty twisted thinking, but he saw it was mainly those bastards who worked hard at being sycophants that managed to move up the various ladders to success. A pretty questionable success as far as he was concerned.

This time though, he felt it would be sloppy—if not downright stupid—to have some con game perpetrated upon him and his friends, without at least trying to find out what the hell was going on.

Georgia was walking out the door of her unit when he arrived.

'Hi,' she said. 'What are you doing here?'

He gave her a lecherous smile. 'Oh no,' she said. 'No time for shenanigans.'

'Joking,' he said.

'Well what do you want?'

'Can we talk inside?'

'I'm dressed,' she said. 'And I'm off to work.'

'No, I'm serious.'

Back inside the unit he put his proposition directly.

'You know we've talked about this raid being a bullshit act.'

She nodded. 'But what can we do about it?'

'Well, Special Operations tends to order people around and put limits on what happens while they're around.'

'Yes, I gathered that.'

'Well, while we're in the bloody house we may as well have a good look around. Check his files. Run off stuff from his computer hard discs. Snoop around generally.'

'I'm for all that.'

'Well,' Mickey said. 'You're more likely to be able to get away with it than any of the rest of us.'

'Us?'

'OK, the men.'

'How's that?'

'Because those mugs in Special Ops tend to think that women don't do anything much that could be important. They won't be watching you. And if they are they won't expect you to be doing anything you weren't told to do.'

Georgia plumped herself down into a chair. 'This is really terrific. Did you think it all out yourself?'

'You know I'm right.'

'All right, so I sneak around picking up everything in range—'

'More than that, you take in a satchel and you open it up in the middle of the floor and say "OK, everything in here." With luck at least half of them will throw stuff in. Even if they don't, we do.'

'So what are we after?'

'All his mates. If they grab his betting books all we get is him. No-one else. I know Travis thinks we'll get his contacts, but if they're smart enough with their laundering there'll be no names. Betting on course is completely anonymous unless it's on credit. My bet is that they do it all with anonymous bets.'

'OK, I like it, I'm in. Is anyone else?'

'I know Ridgy will be. And Frog hated his old man's graft so much he'll be in anything that gives him some revenge on the big boys.' Mickey supposed it was time to go but he wasn't making any move to the door.

'We've got half an hour,' Georgia said. 'It doesn't have to be a marathon event.'

They struggled out of their clothes and climbed under the sheet. 'This might be our last time,' Mickey said. 'Anything could happen today,' he added with some mockery.

'You bloody dag,' Georgia said.

Six

Georgia was excited. She was looking forward to this raid. She wasn't sure whether it was because she was totally accepted as an equal in the field by Mickey, or just the thought of mischievously causing trouble for some of the criminal hierarchy of the city.

As she was passing the office she called to Frog who was collecting his keys. 'Yeah?' he replied.

'Ridgy told me you had a dream. About somebody being shot.'

'Ah, forget it,' Frog laughed. 'I just told them that.'

'You made it up?'

'Yeah.'

Obviously I'm not the only one wanting to play games, she thought.

'Well I *did* have a dream,' she said.

'Don't tell anyone,' Frog said. 'They worry people more than I thought.'

'It was a good dream,' Georgia said. Frog laughed with her.

Georgia was a pretty good observer, and to fill in the time while they drove to Wilson's place in the plumber's van she covertly watched the others. Mickey seemed more precise than usual in his driving. The van flew, well balanced and moving with the right revs. Ridgy was laid back, but she intuited that he was hiding some real tension. He seemed to be acting a part, going through the motions of responding in a reasonable way.

Angel was rubbing his hands down between his knees, the action presumably diverting some of the anticipation. It was the sort of movement that was right for cold days, but it looked rather odd on a warm Sydney afternoon.

Frog was leaning back in his seat opposite the sliding door, his hands intertwined and resting on his stomach. He might have been smoking a pipe in front of a fire. Had he really dreamt that one of them had been shot, or did he like causing ripples of consternation?

And she observed herself. Her tension contained something sexual, and she guessed all excitement did for everyone, although most people would deny it. Or was it just her? No, it had been Mickey that alerted her to the possibilities before they left for work. His loitering had contained a potent message.

Parked across the road from Wilson's place, relying on the timing of his arrival given by Travis, they listened on the radio to the banter of the troops surrounding the place.

Georgia was thinking that if Wilson didn't turn up there was clearly more than one current of crookedness in the force. Any one of those currents would have nullified the games of the other. Then she concluded that she couldn't just guess this stuff, she had to play absolutely objectively here because it would be so easy to fly off on wrong tangents. Her brief period in Vice had alerted her to corruption. Petty stuff really, everyone else said, just some stupid coppers getting involved in the running of brothels, but it was enough to make her request a transfer to Rescue.

* * *

Vic Wilson was in a foul mood. He had wanted to take the seaplane trip with the others to the restaurant on the banks of the Hawkesbury River, but he had to do this stupid clerking job because he couldn't trust any of his employees to do it properly.

He ran the Mercedes hard around the long crescent to his house, hoping Annie Fowler had decided to do a few of the things he wanted done. If she hadn't she was out. There was plenty of other young stuff around. As he approached the gates to his place he felt a ridiculous urge to drive through them, smash everything he had. He slowed the car to give the gates time to open. 'I don't want this shit to take more than an hour, Jack,' he said. 'I want to get out of here.'

He drove too fast up the drive and skidded the big car to a halt, sliding it in the gravel. Annie walked from the house in a leisure gown split to the waist. She smiled at him and he ignored her, although he was pleased she was about. She continued on her way to the pool.

As he walked up the steps to the house he turned back and saw Jack watching Annie with a smile on his face. 'Jack, do you want this bloody job or not?' Vic had never trusted Jack. His eyes scouted around all over the place, always looking for the main chance because he couldn't see it was staring him in the face.

'Sure, Vic.'

'Just keep away from the fuckin' help.'

'Sure, Vic.'

There were four pairs of field glasses focused on this little exchange but none of the observers could lip read, so they could only imagine the two men were talking about the races, about cooking the books, or conspiring to commit further felonies.

Sergeant Travis looked down at his watch. They'd give them five minutes to get down to the bunker and begin work. He called Ridgy giving the new estimated time for the commencement of the raid.

'OK,' Ridgy replied, 'But we'll tell you when to move. We have a clear view of the front of the house, and we've got the first part of the operation.' He put down the handset. 'It's always the simplest things that you don't make allowances for. Happens every time.'

Vic and Jack were making their way down to the basement. One of the guards was knocking balls about by himself in the pool room, and the other was sitting in front of the bank of screens connected to the security cameras. Vic passed them without speaking, although he threw a glowering glance at the bloke attending the surveillance screens because he was reading a book. Briefly he wondered whether Annie had been entertaining herself with these two pricks. This was the main problem for those who knew the extent of their own knavery: they were constantly suspicious of those who were the closest to them. A nice private hell, Vic had, soundly constructed and luxuriously outfitted.

In the bunker Vic realised with annoyance how much he relied on Jack. The bastard knew computers, as well as having one of those masterly mathematical brains. 'Get the figures up,' he said, gesturing at the computer in a way which would alert the technically knowledgeable that he couldn't do it himself. He was a thug by nature and inclination, and such a mentality tends to dissolve when faced with problems of a technical or novel nature.

Jack placed the lightweight case on a desk and flicked it open. He took out the book that recorded the day's bets and walked with it to the computer desk. Vic was taking the counterfeit book from a small safe. He became suddenly aware of the reason he was getting so angry on race days. He was totally in the hands of another person. He saw too, Jack's arrogance around him was growing daily.

* * *

'Sixty seconds,' Ridgy said.

'Keep fiddling those books, Vic,' Mickey said.

'Oh no!' Georgia said. 'Here comes a bloody tourist bus.'

The huge vehicle blocked their view for a moment and went on around the crescent leaving the voice of the tourist guide floating above the panel van: 'On the left is the three point five million dollar residence of well-known racing identity, Vic Wilson.'

'Was the valuation before the bunker or after?' Mickey said.

'Twenty-five seconds,' Ridgy said.

Frog leaned forward to pull the sliding door open. Angel took a firmer grip on his oxyacetylene gear. Mickey touched the butt of his handgun and Georgia raised the empty bag from the floor for the umpteenth time.

'Ten seconds,' Ridgy said.

At the pool, Annie Fowler slipped off her robe to

reveal even more of her, picked up a walkman and sauntered over to the rubberised air-bed bumping against the steps that led into the water.

In the van Ridgy looked right and left for a positive all clear. 'OK, let's go.'

Frog swept open the door and the crew were out and running.

Mickey carried a short ladder. He placed it against the wall to one side of the gate. Georgia and Mickey held it steady while one of Travis's marksmen ran to the top of it, his head hidden by foliage. He was carrying the dart gun to dispose of the dogs.

The dogs were nowhere to be seen. 'Where are the bastards?' the marksman said to himself, but Georgia heard, and raised her eyebrows at Mickey.

'Whistle them,' Mickey said.

'Smart-arse,' the marksman said.

Angel and Frog connected the oxyacetylene equipment and were ready to light up. 'Hurry up.' Frog said, 'Someone will ring him just to be neighbourly.'

Mickey chuckled. 'They didn't really think about the dogs. Didn't take them into account.' Mickey couldn't understand why he was no longer tense. Probably because they were only ancillaries in this one. The responsibility was with someone else. No, that wasn't the point. He had always taken the action aboard personally. It had to be something else. It could only be because he didn't believe in it. The whole thing was a staged event. If they were serious they would never have forgotten that dogs were completely unreliable, that they could be lying under a bush somewhere taking it easy on a warm afternoon, the very moment you wanted them close to fire

76

on. He winked at Frog. Frog raised his eyes to the sky. They had colluded too soon—the dart gun went *phut*. 'Got him,' the marksman said.

'What about the other one?' Frog said. He smiled at Mickey.

'I don't believe you bastards,' Angel said. 'Why don't we go in and kill the bloody dog?'

'Aah, come on Angel,' Frog said. 'Hurt a pup like that?' A dog's loud, savage bark made Angel jump.

Phut went the gun.

The marksman jumped, followed by Mickey, Georgia, and then Frog and Angel, balancing their equipment.

The dogs were stretched out in full view of the house, and they didn't look as if they were sleeping. Georgia and Mickey took one each and dragged them behind some shrubbery. The dogs felt dead. There was a flutter of a front paw from one, as if it were dreaming of pursuing attackers, and then it was still. Georgia and Mickey had to run to catch up with Angel and Frog. Then Mickey split away to wait for Ridgy.

The front door was ornate, with marvellous three-dimensional elaborations of steel grapevines. The art was to disguise the real function of the door—to keep out armed men.

Georgia hooked a slide of gel over the lens of the camera on the porch, and then ran to the others at each end of the building. By the time she was back Angel had fired the torch and was halfway through the bars of the windows on one side of the door. She saw that Mickey and Ridgy had gone the swimming pool route.

Mickey was glad they had. Annie was floating on

the air-bed. She was gently stroking her breasts through the scanty fabric of her swimwear, oblivious to any other activity around her. She felt cocooned by wealth, sensation and music. Annie assumed that men would always be good to her—despite some painful experiences to the contrary—and thus she was not alarmed when she opened her eyes and saw two men in white overalls crouched beside the shrubbery by the fence of the pool. She removed her sunglasses for a closer look. The handsome one smiled at her, gave a little wave, and turned slightly so she read Police Rescue, on the back of his overalls. Mickey thought it was delightful the way she moved her lips as she read.

She gave an embarrassed little smile about what she'd been doing—well, maybe they'd seen her—and waved as they ran off to the house, the handsome one still smiling at her. She really liked him.

Inside the house the guard charged with watching the bank of monitors looked up from his book. It was *Thirst for Love* by Yukio Mishima, and he had bought it because he thought it might be a Japanese version of *Deep Throat*. Getting over his disappointment he read the book with interest. It dealt with all the little things about love that he felt; the kids were specially right. He obviously hadn't finished it.

'Hey, Greg' he called to the other guard. 'All the monitors are on the blink. Must be a fault in the central nervous system, or something.'

'Fault be buggered,' said Greg, grabbing for the Anschutz auto, 'we're being raided.' He had used gel himself in several bank robberies. He slammed the alarm button to the bunker, and ran to the observation window. Instantly he saw two bastards coming from the pool area. He fired two shots from the hip. Christ, coppers! Well, he certainly wouldn't be aiming to hit any. He'd shoot off a few rounds to impress Vic, and when they got into the house he'd whack himself with the barrel, draw blood and collapse on the floor. No way he was going to take on the police force. He knew Vic. The bastard would claim he was an intruder who had nothing to do with him. He'd go up for ten years and be paid to keep his gob shut, or else!

Whirling around he saw that Pete, the monitor guard, had disappeared from his chair in front of the bank of screens. He quickly wiped his fingerprints from the Anschutz and slid it under the pool table. He'd say Pete fired the shots. Burnt powder, he suddenly remembered, and ran to the bathroom to wash his hands and face. They could trace anything these days.

Having done all that he came out to the pool table again, and standing with his hands on the edge brought his head down as hard as he dared. I did it too haaaar—, he thought, as he collapsed. And he'd be out for even longer than he anticipated because he fell backwards and his head caught the hearth in front of the fireplace.

Georgia came through the house, her thirty-eight special held at shoulder height. She had the bag on her back. Behind her were Angel and Frog carrying the gear. The Special Operations morons had disappeared. They'd run ahead like motorcycle cops who outdistance the limo they are escorting.

In the centre of the courtyard they saw the skylight for the bunker. The glass was contained in a cage with the bar density of a wicker basket. Frog nudged Angel. 'It'd be easier than cutting through the door.'

'Depends how it's held in place,' Angel said.

Frog ran out and checked. He held four fingers up to Angel. Four bolts. Angel waved Georgia back from her position further along the hall. She realised instantly what they were about. 'We need Travis's mob to go through first,' she said. 'I have no idea where they are.'

'We'll leave the gear here, and go and look for them. A steel door will take an hour to get through if it's remotely like the front. All those locks and supports.'

In the bunker Vic Wilson had his shredder going. He was wishing he'd gone for the bigger model. It had been the salesman's fault that he hadn't. He was such a smug bastard, smirking, as if he knew Vic would need the really big model. Vic had gone for the little model to teach the bastard a lesson.

This way it was going to take him ten minutes to dispose of everything. He was ripping the pages out of the genuine betting book ten at a time. He looked at Jack who was standing with his mouth open. 'You soft bastard,' he yelled. 'Take the shottie and keep them off me for as long as you can. I don't care how you do it.'

You've got to be joking, Jack thought. I care. I'm out of here. I'll go through the hedge at the back of the tennis court. That was where he sneaked in to rendezvous with Annie when Vic was out for the night. It was an area unobserved by the surveillance cameras.

Jack took the shotgun and ran out. Vic slid the bolts home on the steel door. They'd have to be too late now. No bastard was going to get through. There was one thing about Jack, he could be relied on.

A few seconds later there was a mighty banging on the door. The double-crossing bastard, he thought. He's shot through. OK, calm down he told himself, I'm ahead now. When the clowns burst through there'll be nothing to find. Just keep the fingers out of the shredder. Don't stuff it too full. Don't jam it. Do it properly.

Outside, the Special Operations mob refused to change their plan again. They said they had been told only a few minutes before the raid began that they would go in through the bunker door. 'But it'll only be a few minutes if you go in through the top,' Georgia explained. 'That's what the original plan was.' There was a plea in her voice. Frog was sceptical. 'Leave them. You won't change them. I'll get the stuff.'

As far as Vic was concerned, they weren't just going through the motions. He hadn't known about any raid and he was in strong with the cops. He was going to tear some livers out after this. He had been paying plenty to avoid this sort of shit. Someone was trying to teach him a lesson.

OK, he told himself, I'm ready for them. He sat down on the chair in front of the computer and spun it around to the door. He would smile when they came through. Then a terrible thought struck him. The computer. God, the secrets it held. He turned back to look at. The stupid bloody thing. The great eye of it was looking at him with a list of phoney bets. Well, at least that was all right. But somewhere in there was the genuine stuff. Cool down, he warned himself. Jack puts a disc in with all the information on it. He's always talking about discs, booting it up, that sort of stuff. Jesus he'd like to give it a bloody boot now. Right, so if I did smash it the disc would still be in there. I'll take the disc out and smash it.

He removed the disc and was about to drop it on the floor, when it suddenly dawned on him it would be stupid to destroy all the information. It would be lost forever. He couldn't use it to call in favours. Vic had cooled himself out too much. Confident Vic, they called him. Still holding the disc he stepped onto the table, reached down and pulled up a chair, and stood on it, which took him up into the glass skylight. He opened it a fraction and gave the disc a little push, so it would nicely balanced there, out of harm's way.

Georgia had been fascinated by the skylight and the barred cage over it. It was a terrible weakness. If someone gained entrance to the house, and knew about the bunker, all they had to do was break the glass and toss gas or fireworks through it—and it was goodnight Vic. Georgia had assumed all visitors to the house would be trying to kill him.

As she stared at the glass she saw one side of it move slightly. She bent down just as Vic nudged the disc out. 'Thanks,' she said in a whisper as she leaned forward and picked it up. If Vic had hesitated on the chair top a moment longer he would have heard the whisper. Not that it would have done him any good. He would just have known a few minutes earlier that he was in deep shit.

Georgia was very satisfied with herself as she followed Frog and Angel down to the bunker with the gear. Unfortunately for the guard who read Mishima,

Georgia was interested in the bedroom in the mansion. With her handgun hanging down by her side, and the computer disc safely in her pocket, she opened one of the doors. The room had a palatial air. The carpet was lush and thick. The huge wardrobes were made from highly polished walnut, and the bed was a complete circle. Above the bed was suspended a huge mirror. She gazed up into the looking-glass. How would I look on such a bed? she asked herself. Maybe a Renoir with muscles. But there was something else reflected in the mirror.

She thought it strange that a silken bed cover should have a rather shabby boot emerging from beneath it. She retreated behind the door, glanced down the hallway to discover if she was alone, and then demanded that the boot reveal its contents. 'I know you're under the bed and if you don't move out, face down, crawling on your belly with your hands on the back of your head, I'll blow your ankle to pieces.'

The man—it was Pete, the screen monitor—moved out, undulating on his belly. Georgia stood him against the wall and searched him. No firearms.

Walking behind him she guided him towards the bunker. At the end of the hall the guard's body became two. The other guard, Greg, dazed on waking, had forgotten his grand plan for maintaining his innocence, and decided to run for it. Flying out of the billiard room and still looking over his shoulder, he bounced off Pete, hit the wall and kept coming.

Georgia tried to step to one side, but she was knocked down. She could have shot the guard but decided against it. She had no trace of desire to shoot anyone. There was not even the consideration that she might be regarded as a hero or, at the very least, a person at the centre of press attention—until an inquiry was completed.

Pete had no confidence in escape and no wish to incriminate himself further. He sat down to wait for justice to claim him.

Meanwhile, Greg had Georgia firmly pinned. He was sitting astride her with a hand pinning each of her wrists to the floor. One of Georgia's hands still held the pistol. The guard was still calculating whether he could leave one of her wrists loose while he grabbed for the gun, because it was obvious she would twist her body quickly. He felt in no condition to wrestle with a body that felt so marvellously muscled.

He needn't have worried. Mickey bent down beside him and whispered, 'That's a funny position to be in, mate. Now if you wouldn't mind, I'd like you to rise slowly to the standing position.' The muzzle of Mickey's thirty-eight special probed the soft neck.

The guard concentrated on that sensation in his neck because he knew it was important that he do so. The muzzle was colder than the surrounding air, but it still didn't impose itself completely on his mind-numbing headache. He pleaded with Mickey. 'Please help me up. I'm just the butler here, and someone struck me about the head.'

'If you're the butler,' Mickey said, 'why are you sitting on my girlfriend?'

'Mickey!' Georgia warned.

'Sorry sweetheart, it's just my jealous nature.'

Georgia pushed the guard away, and he fell to one side in slow motion.

As Georgia and Mickey were deciding what to do with the two guards they were surprised by Frog and Angel and the Special Operations team returning. 'They've finally decided to believe they won't get through the door for an hour or so,' Angel said.

'Yeah,' Frog said.

The whole contingent repaired to the courtyard. Angel lit the torch and went for the skylight. Each bolt took about thirty seconds. Four burly Special Operations men stepped forward and lifted the cage from the glass.

Another smashed the glass with a rifle butt. It shattered in the style of safety glass, and Travis and another dropped through the skylight.

Vic was waiting for them. He clapped them loudly. 'Very good,' he said. 'Very, very good.'

Travis looked at the basket below the shredding machine, while his colleague unbolted the steel bars that made the door so impregnable.

Georgia was the first through the door. 'All right,' she said, throwing the open bag on the floor, 'everything in here.'

'Now wait a minute,' Travis said. 'We're taking all this stuff.'

'Where's your bag?' Georgia said.

'OK,' Travis allowed, 'but we take the bag.'

'It's not up to me,' Georgia said. 'It's up to the senior rank on the job.'

'Bullshit,' Travis said.

Noting that he was no longer the centre of attention, Vic began to move towards the door. Confronted by a team of blokes in gas masks, their masks turning them into alien animals, he leaned back on the wall next to the door while they entered, and then left behind them. He knew people behind gas masks are completely disoriented. Like those with tunnel vision, they cannot have confidence in what they see. They can be led. Anything out of sight of their pebble-sized viewing sockets, is also out of mind.

Vic was free in his hallway. Imagining they would expect him to run from the house he decided to hide himself in the roof, and ran for the stairs to the second storey.

Mickey, coming from the rear of the house, heard the sudden commotion from the basement as it was realised Vic was gone. Realising the bastard hadn't run to the back of the house and thus the entrance to the garage, Mickey also calculated he wouldn't be running out the front door in plain view of the assembled Special Operations squad. That meant up-stairs. No-one followed Mickey. The rest were sure he would attempt to escape from the house, and ran for the front or the back.

Upstairs was quiet. The carpets were thick enough to deaden the sound of a trotting horse. The place was still. Light was constant. That impressed Mickey. Light in small houses was affected by every waving branch or passing cloud. The roof, Mickey thought, he'll hide in the roof. At least he won't have any idea I'm coming. We're going to surprise each other.

Openings to the roof generally tended to be in ceilings or in cupboards. Mickey looked in the first room, and noted it was lined with cupboards.

He convinced himself it would be better to check all the rooms quickly, and then double back to check the cupboards. If there was an escape route to the roof, Vic would already be there.

And there in the master bedroom, was Vic, loading a shotgun by the window. Without a thought, Mickey launched himself, sprinting silently across the carpet. Vic sensed it, flicking the double barrels closed as he turned. Vic was fast. He had the sort of reflexes Mickey had. Mickey knew he had to hit him harder than he'd ever hit anyone. Giving him a second chance at levelling the shotgun could be fatal. Mickey's rush took them through the French doors and over the knee-high balcony. Both barrels of the shotgun exploded harmlessly as they were descending in mid-air, but the pattern of the blast accompanying their falling bodies made a marvellous spectacle.

The pool saved them. They went in the deep end.

Annie Fowler saw them explode through the doors. The shotgun emptied its two loads of heavy shot into the pool, close enough to her to graze her sun tan, the sound cracking through even her walkman ear pieces. She saw the handsome cop turn Vic in midair and ride him down so that Vic's back took the brunt of the water surface. As the waves overturned her air-bed, she winced for Vic. A back-flop would be as bad as a belly-flop. Cool droplets from the spray of the impact sprinkled her hot skin. The cop's head emerged first. He gave her a pleasant smile as he hauled Vic to the side of the pool. He seemed to be about to pull Vic out, but then changed his mind and held his head under. Annie wondered if she had been going with Vic long enough for him to have included her in his will. She didn't think so. The handsome cop smiled at her again as he raised Vic's head and pushed it under a second time.

When Mickey lifted Vic's head the third time he saw that the bastard could even think under water. His eyes were steady. 'Fuck you,' Vic said to Mickey. He knew no cop was going to drown him—not in front of witnesses. Mickey let him go and waited for him to climb out.

Vic sprang out of the pool. 'Get me the senior man,' he said to Mickey. Mickey realised the bastard was replenishing his spirit from some hidden reserve. As they started back for the house, they were surrounded by Travis's men. Back in the mansion, Vic was demanding his phone call.

Ridgy nodded yes to Mickey, and Vic picked up his portable phone from the sideboard and dialled his lawyer's number from memory. A close relationship here.

'Vic Wilson here, tell Frank . . . no I'll wait.' Wilson turned to Ridgy and Travis. 'Can you tell me why honest, hard working people like me are always harassed by cowboy coppers like you? I have connections in this state, Sergeant. And you might find yourself on point duty in, let's say, aah, Tipaburra?' Vic turned back to the phone. 'I don't care *what* he's in, get him out. I keep your firm afloat and he knows it. Tell him it's Vic Wilson, and it's urgent. I tell you what,' he added to Ridgy and Travis. 'This bloke's gonna chop you into little pieces.'

'Only if he pays the right politicians,' Ridgy said.

'He'll do that all right.'

'Did you all hear that,' Ridgy said. 'Vic Wilson here

said his lawyer would bribe politicians to get him off any charges.'

'Frank!' Vic suddenly yelled down the phone. 'I've got the bloody Girl Guides at the house and I want you to get down here now.' Vic listened for a moment and then grinned. 'Frank wants to talk to one of you,' he said, handing the phone to Ridgy, who handed it to Travis.

'Sergeant Travis here.' Travis listened, and his face hardened.

'He'll be taken and charged at the city watch-house,' was all he said, and handed the phone back to Vic.

Vic walked away a few steps. Travis asked Mickey if he had told him his rights.

'Certainly did,' Mickey said. 'Started on the way down, and finished under water.'

'Be serious,' Travis said.

'No,' Mickey said.

'We can't use the stuff about the politicians then.'

'I don't know,' Ridgy said. 'A good lawyer would get it before the jury somehow.'

A Special Operations member staggered into the front hall with Vic's computer. 'You can't have that,' Vic yelled and appeared to grab for it. It fell to the floor, and when it was picked up again the innards of it seemed to rattle and move. Vic smiled.

'OK,' Travis said to Vic, 'let's go.'

A few minutes later Georgia came into the hallway. Her bag was pretty much full and Frog went to take one side of it.

'Nice dive,' Georgia said to Mick.

89

'What have you got there?' Ridgy asked.

'A lot of stuff. I don't know how good it is though. He's shredded everything he thought was evidence. And if there was anything on hard disc, it's gone.' Georgia looked at Mickey and winked.

Ridgy said, 'Everyone be sure of what you did and where you did it. This is gonna be ugly. You got everything. Now Special Ops will contact us later when Travis remembers the stuff in the bag. He's obviously forgotten about it at the moment. I want everything we give them listed.'

Annie Fowler was still floating in the pool. She watched the four-wheel drive vehicles leave. 'I can stay here,' she thought. 'This is my house for a while. I can do anything I want here. Vic didn't even say goodbye.' She back-paddled the air-bed to the pool steps, wondered if the broken glass had scattered this far, twisted off the air-bed which now floated out to the middle of the pool, and walked on tippie-toes to the open doors.

Back at the depot Georgia caught Mickey outside the locker room. 'I've got the disc that was in the computer. Wilson pushed it out the skylight to me.'

'He *what*?'

'He didn't know I was there. I suppose he thought he was hiding it.'

'Brilliant. Bloody brilliant, Georgie. OK, when we give a report to Adams you use the computer to copy all the information onto another disc. He'll be out of his office for about ten minutes. It probably won't take you that long.'

'Jesus, Mickey, this is serious stuff, copying evidence. And what if he catches me, what do I do then?'

'You can tell him anything you want. He's one of the old school. He's never trusted computers. A virus could be destroying the data bank right before his eyes and he wouldn't know.'

'No-one would,' Georgia said.

'Georgia we need this. There is not a problem provided ... aah, yeah, I'll tell you what I'll do. Follow me.'

Mickey knocked on Adams's door. 'Inspector,' he began, 'I take it you'll want copies of everything we have before we hand it over to Special Ops. You know, just in case they lose anything, if you know what I mean.'

'None of that bullshit,' Adams said to Mickey. 'Copy it, sure, but let's not run around jumping to conclusions on anything, right?'

Georgia pushed Mickey aside. 'I'll just copy this disc. It's probably nothing, but you never know.'

'Hold it,' Adams said. 'Now I don't mind you copying stuff, but I don't want any trouble, right? No competition with another squad. No innuendo.' And he waved Georgia into his office.

Georgia went to the computer desk, took two new discs from the drawer and placed them to one side near the B drive. She slipped Vic's disc into A drive and copied the files onto the hard disc. She then took one new disc, slipped it into B and copied all the documents onto that. She took it out and repeated the process with the other new disc. She smiled at Adams who was watching her suspiciously, but without any real understanding, then picked up the three discs and left the room.

'Make sure the stuff goes to Special Ops,' Adams called after her.

She turned and smiled her confirmation.

After they had packed the vans again, Adams strolled out for a casual briefing. Mickey was already asleep on his favourite bench and didn't hear a word. No-one bothered to wake him.

Later, at Georgia's, Mickey watched her place the disc into her personal computer. 'It's on a different program,' she said, 'but mine can interpret it.' Mickey watched, amazed, as the words flashed on the screen that the material on the disc was from an alien program, but that it was already interpreting it. Please wait.

Once the translations were complete Georgia began calling up the documents on file. They contained the names of the men and organisations who backed the winning horses—several hours after the races were over. The expected names were there, including several large developers who were obviously getting their seed money from drugs, and laundering it with Vic before putting it to work for them. Mickey followed the process as Georgia described it.

'After selling the drugs for cash,' Georgia explained, 'they give the money to Vic, who holds it until he's entered up the phoney bets in his books. He then gives it back to them as money they have supposedly legitimately won at the races. Occasionally you see these huge winnings mentioned in the newspapers. This gives the money more credibility. With this "clean" money they begin their developments.'

Instead of the high they had expected from discovering the secrets of the disc, Mickey and Georgia became depressed. This was impossible material to work through. A lot of the people named in the documents helped run the state. The media observed and wrote about them on a daily basis. The state wouldn't be so prosperous without them.

An hour later they walked out of Georgia's unit and down to the local bar on the waterfront. No wonder Vic had put in a bunker. He needed protection. It was a wonder it hadn't been even further fortified. Like its own air supply, a moat with crocodiles, and special walls with advancing spikes to dispose of unwanted visitors.

Sipping their drinks, and looking out over Pittwater towards Scotland Island, they remained with their own thoughts for a time, comfortably silent.

'Well,' Mickey speculated. 'Plenty of people could have wanted that raid, specially if they had known he was using real names instead of a code. I mean, he was probably blackmailing some of them. You know, continuing the operation because *they* needed it, but getting more and more of a percentage for himself.'

Georgia saw an even grander scenario. 'They couldn't just kill him, unless they could be absolutely sure of destroying all that incriminating evidence. How could they be sure? You can bet he'd be protecting his back. With that sort of extortion running for him, he could really have begun running the state. He could have asked favours of all of them.'

'What do we do with it then, the information?' Mickey asked. He was lost simply trying to comprehend the enormity of it all.

'We go to the major crime squad,' Georgia said.

'Christ, no,' Mickey exclaimed. 'They've always been

on the take. Just ask Frog. His old man set it all up.'

'We could just wait and see what Special Ops does with it. I mean, they have it all too. They've got the same dilemma.'

'Do you want to make any bets on this one?' Mickey asked.

'No,' Georgia paused. 'But you see what I mean don't you, about Vic having the clout to run the state? He's only got to have the guts to say: right, everyone does what I say, otherwise I don't do any more laundering, and I hand over the books for immunity.'

'That's probably what he'll do anyway.'

'Has there ever in the history of the world,' Georgia began, 'been an inquiry that accused all the top dogs, and sent any of them to the slammer?'

'I think it happened in Victoria,' Mickey said. 'They cleaned up their act for a while, but it's different now. All the coppers there freelance, whereas here it's . . .'

'Institutionalised?'

'Yeah, that.' Mickey said.

Seven

Georgia and Mickey looked out over the ocean at Dee Why. The waves were really booming in, spray curling back from the breakers like long, wind-swept hair. It was an awesome sight. They were travelling back to the depot after rescuing a baby from a locked car. Anyone could have done it with a coat hanger or plastic binder twine, but the police had been called, probably because the caller thought the mother deserved a lecture. She hadn't got one. She had been so distraught it would have been inappropriate.

'Don't you find it funny?' Georgia said.

'What's funny?' Mickey asked.

'Well, we're working on these little rescues, and all the while we're sitting on Vic's information that could put away most of the state's top crims, not to mention expose a lot of so-called respectable businessmen.'

'Do we want to sit on it?' Mickey asked. 'It's a real time bomb.'

'Only if the timer's activated. In the meantime, we've got to be sure of the ramifications. I don't want to die just yet.'

'I think we should talk to Ridgy about it. He's got mates in Special Ops and the major crime squad.'

Frog's voice broke in over the radio. 'Rescue Five.'

'Yes, Frog,' Georgia replied.

'Good morning, Constable Rattray, and how are we?'

'We are fine,' Georgia said.

'Well, we have a garbled message about a kid being trapped in a shopping centre near you. Warringah Road, near Dutton Street.'

'Three minutes, Frog,' Georgia said.

Mickey turned the vehicle at the next set of lights. 'On the other hand, I don't think we should talk to Ridgy just yet. He seems to have another problem.'

'Gina?'

'Yeah, he's completely gone on her. I don't know about her, though.'

'I thought she'd go for Angel.'

'You mean because you would?'

'Of course,' Georgia said. 'I've been in love with the little spunk since the first moment I clapped eyes on him.' She looked at Mickey. 'Are you satisfied? Does that knock your ego around enough?'

Mickey laughed. 'The problem is, I don't know if you're fair dinkum or not.'

'If I was fair dinkum, I'd certainly have slept with him by now.'

'What do you mean?'

'That's what I mean.' She changed the subject. 'Gina likes older blokes though. I talked to her about it. The young ones bore her. They're all red hot but they lose the plot, and they don't really know what they want.'

'That's pretty heavy stuff,' Mickey said. 'Do women really talk about men so ... crudely?'

'You mean dismissively, don't you? In the way men talk about women.'

96

'Yeah, I suppose I do.'

Mickey spun the vehicle into the shopping centre car park.

They couldn't miss the crowd outside the antique shop. Georgia approached the window where the shoppers milled around. Georgia was surprised by what she saw. 'A puppy,' she exclaimed, quite delighted by the little thing prancing around as if it knew it was the entertainer. She tapped on the window, and it looked at her, its head cocked to one side. 'It's gorgeous,' she said to the assembled crowd.

'He's been in there two days,' said a woman with two heavy string bags.

Georgia followed Mickey to the rear of the premises.

Mickey tried the window and it slipped up easily. Georgia was the first through. In the front of the shop the puppy heard them and turned around to look. When it saw Georgia coming, it performed a little dance, wagging its tail furiously. Georgia picked it up and the onlookers outside cheered and clapped.

Back at the depot Ridgy saw the pup in Georgia's arms. 'Is that the victim?' he asked.

'That's right,' Georgia said.

'Some victim,' Mickey said. 'He ate half the antique shop.'

'Oh, he's just hungry,' Georgia said.

'Did you see the news?' Ridgy asked.

'What news?' Mickey asked.

'About Vic Wilson,' Ridgy said. Georgia swung around, making the puppy's head lurch so wide it yelped. 'They've let him go,' Ridgy said.

'I don't believe it,' Georgia said. 'You're joking?'

'Nope,' Ridgy said.

'But the material we sent them,' Mickey said. 'It's too blatant to just let him go. What does Adams say?'

'What should he say?' Ridgy asked.

Mickey was silent, looking at Ridgy. You know what I mean.

'We know what you mean,' Frog said from his seat.

'Well that disc names everyone who is laundering big money in this town,' Mickey said.

'You didn't tell me about any disc,' Ridgy said.

'Well, it wasn't our business,' Georgia said. 'Until now.'

'Have we got a copy?' Frog asked.

'On the computer,' Georgia said, nodding towards Adams's office.

'Well, what do we do about it?' Frog asked. 'Are we really knights?'

Mickey knocked on Adams's door and entered.

'Hear they let Wilson go,' Mickey said. 'Seems like they wasted our time.'

'They always do, don't they?' Adams replied.

Georgia entered behind Mickey. 'I had a peep at the material on that disc we gave them, and it had all the names of the people laundering money through his system.'

'It was up to the major crime squad to act on the evidence,' Adams said. 'It appears that they didn't think there was enough to go on.'

'Well you have a look at it,' Georgia said. 'I put a copy on our hard disc.'

'Not any more. I had Gina remove a lot of stuff the other day.'

'You're kidding!'

'Yeah. She told me the hard disc was getting pretty

full. I asked her to check if you'd put any more stuff on it. That's all. I mean, I thought you probably would've saved it automatically. You didn't mention it to me. I don't know how these things work.'

Georgia smiled. 'Yeah, I thought this sort of thing might happen—them letting him go, I mean. And I *did* save it because we were copying everything.' She looked over at Mickey who was staring at Adams open mouthed.

She knew she was treading the dainty line between honesty and downright deception, but she was worried that if she was completely honest, admitted she did have further copies, that they might be requested. For a moment she was going to accuse Adams of . . . something.

Her sense of diplomacy won out. Larger currents were moving here. A display of anger would reveal her hand; place her on an unwanted list. Mickey hadn't said anything. Perhaps the old boar was just teasing her. 'Well that's it then,' she said. 'I thought we could make it more official somehow. If they knew we had the material—'

'It would be dangerous,' Adams finished off her sentence, nodding at her: yes, that's how it is.

'Are you sure, Bill?' Mickey asked. 'That's condemning a lot of people.'

'What are you talking about?' Adams said. 'I haven't accused anyone of anything.'

'Bullshit,' Mickey said.

'Look Mickey, I put up with you because you're a terrific craftsman. You can get anybody out of anywhere. You can save people. But that's the only reason. I don't see you as a great crime fighter. We

99

all know what goes on in this city. The blokes on the major squads tiptoe around the edges of what's going on.'

'I see,' Georgia said, and backed out the door, closing it. She saw Mickey settle with his rump on Adams's desk. The old bastard was going to convince Mickey that nothing could be done. Well, she had it from the boar's mouth. That's how it is. Where did one go from here? She thought for a moment of going to the papers, but one of the names had been a considerable media influence. She understood she was as impotent with this knowledge as anyone she might meet on the street. They all were.

She saw for a moment how Aborigines must feel when they're told their people *weren't* being killed in police cells. Sure, some of the deaths would come from anger, and a suicidal hanging was as brutal a message as any that they had been badly treated. People disfigure themselves in their deaths to express anger. She'd read that. But the other 'hangings', where the bodies appeared badly beaten and were strung up in the most makeshift way, couldn't be explained in the antiseptic and sterile way of inquiry reports. The reports made no acknowledgement or allowance for the capacity of people for brutality and hatred—and plain old-fashioned murder. The investigators simply had no real life experience. They accepted the words of the police witnesses. After all, *they* all appeared quite normal; they were also used to giving evidence in the witness box and adopting the correct attitudes. And they were quick to change their attitudes if they saw their questioners required it.

She sat down in the canteen. Ptomaine brought her

a cup of coffee. She glanced at him. 'Hear you had some success yesterday,' he said. She nodded, giving him a tired smile. Through the door she saw Mickey slip from the table and bang a fist on it. He leaned towards Adams as if he were straining on a leash.

Mickey was outraged at the gutlessness in the force. His words boiled with anger. 'You mean to say we put ourselves at risk every day and not one of you bastards are prepared to do the same. I don't believe it.' He jabbed his finger towards Adams as if he were aiming a handgun. 'You're saying the force is so top heavy with compromise it can't really do a bloody thing about crime. I don't fucking believe I'm hearing this.'

Adams sat down. He was calm, which angered Mickey more. 'Mickey when you get to the age of most senior cops, you're getting tired. You want every promotion you can get, and you're prepared to look the other way to get it. Now listen, I used to condemn the old bastards, Frog's old man, a few others who're still around. They're not bad people, Mickey. They're weak people. They see what's around and they want some of it.'

Mickey saw he'd get nowhere and walked to the door. 'It's all old crooks together, then.' Adams was looking down. 'You can't beat them, Mickey,' he said.

Georgia called Mickey over. 'Isn't it bloody beautiful,' Mickey said. 'Nobody is going to do anything. Wilson walks free, and all his mates are untouched.'

'But something has happened,' Georgia said.

'What do you mean?'

'Wilson no longer holds all the power. The information that gives the power is now with some top cop. Wilson probably ratted on them as well. Maybe that's how it works now: it's somehow all controlled. This is how their power gets clipped—if they get too big they have their feet bound. They can't trample old traditions and still claim the power.' Georgia wasn't sure she put much faith in this theory, but she had to work with Mickey, and she didn't want him without his mind on the job. Others had seen Mickey's performance in Adams's office and now they came drifting in, anxious to know what was going down, but when they saw Mickey and Georgia talking hard they kept to a respectable distance.

'You mean the big rogues have to answer in some way?'

'I'm not sure what I mean. It makes sense of the raid though. It was carried out for *some* reason. It did happen.'

'Maybe it's just a move to get more money out of them.'

'So what do we do with what we've got?'

But that decision had to be put off for another moment. Ridgy entered the canteen. 'Right, you lot. Everyone's on this one. We've got a job down at Wallagarra Valley. And you take your cutting equipment with you.

'You know what it's about. The Greenies are out in force. They're attempting to chain themselves to bulldozers, you know, that sort of stuff. You've done it before. They reckon they're saving the forest ... probably are, but it's our job to get them out of the way. OK, on your way.'

Eight

The river moved with powerful currents, silently. In the huge eucalypts flights of parrots rocketed with unerring accuracy through the foliage high above the surface. This was the Wallagarra Valley. A marvellous piece of wilderness that had never been developed because no-one could get there—until now. Now the yellow bulldozers, that from the air looked for all the world like kids' toys, were making a road through the valley from south to north.

The wide river mouth exchanged water with the ocean and here the sea life had thrived. The water had been clear, the sunlight and oxygen had created their magic. Now the river was muddied, growing more like the mouth of the Cairns River, two thousand kilometres to the north, that spewed out mud from all the denuded hills and sugar-cane plains. North and south of that city swimmers couldn't see their hands an inch beneath the water.

The Rescue vehicles handled the slippery red mud tracks down the valley pretty easily. Mickey, Georgia and Ridgy were in the lead. They rounded the bend to where the confrontation was taking place. Several hundred protesters were milling around a stationary bulldozer. Its motor was still running though, blowing the black diesel smoke of a crook engine. On the side of the dozer some kids had chained themselves to the blade supports.

Mickey and Georgia climbed onto the dozer with their cutters, and cut free the enthusiastic 'prisoners'.

A young girl asked Georgia, 'Why are you going along with these pigs? You know what's going on here.'

'Yeah,' Georgia said. 'Some of us do. But do you think you're doing it the right way?'

Mickey overheard the exchange. 'It won't work, just getting people angry.'

'Nothing works,' the girl said. 'We've been doing it the right way. Put in our submissions, talked to the committees of inquiry, and they just bulldoze us.' She gestured at the dozer they were about to jump from.

Angel and Frog helped the protesters down and marched them to the police van.

'I hate doing this work,' Angel said.

'It's who we're doing it for that pisses me off,' Frog said.

Georgia jumped from the dozer just as the driver chose to jerk it into gear. She knew it was a deliberate move, because she was a woman, and she gave him the finger. Some of the crowd cheered. Georgia wasn't exactly sure who they were cheering.

Mickey was roped in with Angel to remove one of the struggling girls from in front of the dozer. The driver was dangerously inching ahead as each person was removed. Taking the girl's arm by one hand—Angel had her other arm—Mickey waved palm down for the driver to stop the aggro. The driver just stared back at him blankly, as if he thought Mickey was some kind of moron.

Georgia saw that one of the people lying on the ground was an elderly woman. She walked over to her and helped her up. 'I'm not cut out for this,' the woman said. She was stiff and Georgia supported her to a place to sit. 'It's a shame they're going to ruin this gorgeous place,' the woman said.

'Yes, it is,' Georgia said.

'Why do you do it, dear?'

'It's my job,' Georgia replied.

'But they're trying to save the forest for the future.'

Georgia smiled at her and moved away. Could the woman see how shaky her smile was? Mickey walked over to her. 'Now we get to beat up little old ladies.'

The loud hailer seemed impossibly loud, even against the revving of the bulldozer. 'I'm Police Sergeant Ryan, and I'm asking you to move away from the machines now. If you don't you leave yourself open to immediate arrest. Please clear the area now and allow the work to continue.'

Georgia looked at the scene in front of her. The half-made road and the clearing in front of them was a great red dirt scar. Other bulldozers were starting up, belching smoke, and moving in to commence work. The high foliage rippled like a mirage in the heat of the exhausts. She looked at Frog, stopped him with a hand on the shoulder and pointed at the scene as the protesters ran to reform around the dozers. 'We shouldn't be doing this,' she said.

'No, it really stinks,' Frog said.

Ridgy and Mickey heard the conversation as they came up. 'Hey, you bleeding hearts. What would you

105

rather be doing, pulling bodies out of mangled cars?'
Ridgy had no time for concerns of the heart today.
His was still smarting badly.

'Just about,' Mickey said. 'You try arresting people
who are protesting the things you want to protest
against.'

'I have, mate. Every copper has,' Ridgy replied
flatly.

'Doesn't mean we have to like it,' Frog interjected.
'It's gonna look great on the news tonight.'

Georgia was feeling worse every minute about the
ludicrous position they were in. 'Putting a road
through here is criminal. The protesters are absolutely right in what they're doing. We should be
asked whether we want to do this kind of work or not.'

'It ought to be done by volunteers, you mean?'
Ridgy asked.

The dozers came to a stop again as the protesters
reformed. Again the uniformed police moved in.
They had been reinforced. Dust from a dozen or so
paddy wagons coming onto the red scar hung over
the trees. 'Isn't this a bit over the top?' Georgia asked
the rest of the squad, who were watching from the
bank of a cutting.

'They're gonna cart the lot away,' Ridgy said.
'Wholesale arrests.'

Ridgy was about to order them back to work, but
Mickey said, 'Look, we don't have to do anything.
We're just reserves. We came to cut them off the
dozers, that's all. Our work's done.'

Ridgy looked at his squad. 'Rescue isn't a democracy
you know.'

'It sort of is,' Frog said. 'Everyone knows we do

106

work no-one else can, or wants to, so they're a bit indulgent with us. You know what I mean. So we should use that attitude to our advantage. Look what we did for Special Ops the other day, and they knew it was bullshit. We're not on the take. We're honest cops doing the hardest work in the force. You know what I mean, Ridgy. We make them look bad, so they can't touch us.'

Ridgy didn't reply, but smiled and leaned back against a giant tree. There was an imperceptible and resigned shake of his head.

Mickey continued the challenge to Ridgy's passive authority, even though it was no longer necessary. But that was Mickey. 'Why the hell do they want a four lane highway through here anyway? How'd you like one up the back of your place, Ridgy?'

'There *is* a four lane highway at the back of my place,' Ridgy replied.

'You know what I mean,' Mickey said.

'Hey, hey, hey,' Frog said pointing. 'Look what we've got here.'

'Who?' asked Georgia, looking at the three men who had alighted from a rather muddy limo. They wore expensive suits.

'The tall one is Lloyd Prosser, infamous developer and one of the blokes we were going to net in the Vic Wilson raid. The plump little bloke is Darryl Burke. He's the press secretary of the Minister for Development. The third bloke, well, I've seen him around.'

Georgia moved from the bank that the dozers had cut. She leaned a hand to the soil and sprang down. She had a small camera in her hand and she moved closer to the well-dressed trio, ostensibly to photograph the protesters beyond.

The bouncy press secretary, Burke, was waving his arms very expansively. 'Now, it's twelve kilometres from here to the bay. The Minister will be announcing the bay development itself next week. I'm preparing the press release now. He said to assure you the lower valley second stage has also got the go ahead.' Prosser looked at his companion and smiled and nodded.

The unidentified man said, 'I was going to talk to him about that today.'

'Sure, I understand,' Burke said.

'What about these bloody protesters?' Prosser asked.

Burke's smile was smug in his smooth face. His neck protruded as far as his chin, which meant when he stroked his chin he was also stroking a part of his neck. 'Mmm, yes. The police will "quarantine" the whole area, from here to the bay will be a no go area. There'll be nothing to worry about.'

Prosser patted Burke on the back. 'I'd like to see these little pricks roughed up a bit, you know what I mean? What damn right have they got, to hold up an important and expensive development like this? Who do they think they are?'

Burke smiled and scraped the ground with his feet, one after the other. If he was attempting to mimic a bull's gesture before charging, he was well clear of the mark. Prosser patted his shoulder in a patronising way: you know what I'm talking about, hey mate?

Georgia was furious. She had felt like bursting into the conversation, but was glad she had the forebearance to stay silent. She wanted to tell Prosser that she agreed with the protesters that the forest was important. More important than his development scam.

Prosser looked about before returning to the car with his friends. Seeing a good-looking policewoman nearby he smiled and waved. 'You're doing a good job,' he said. 'There'll be a beautiful road through here.'

'Get stuffed,' Georgia said quietly, hoping Prosser was a lip reader.

As the limo turned, Georgia walked back up the steep incline to the others. She knew Prosser had laundered two hundred thousand dollars last week. She knew where his development money was coming from. What could she do with the disc except study it? To alert anyone to her having it could be very dangerous, as Adams had said.

'What were they talking about?' Mickey asked.

'About what good mates they all are—'

'Money always makes good mates,' Frog interjected.

'And how the police should be tougher on the protesters. Prosser was really sure the cops should be tough, you know, as if he had never broken any rules, as if he would never be on the receiving end,' Georgia continued, unable to hold back the sarcasm. The frustration, of having this information and yet being unable to do anything with it, felt paralysing.

Mickey kicked at the red earth. 'The bastards, they get away with everything.'

'Nothing's happening down below,' Ridgy said.

'It's knock-off time,' Frog said. The dozer drivers were walking away from machines, yelling and giving the finger to the protesters. A cheer went up. The protesters had won the day. The trees could have the night again.

They arrived back at the depot around seven. Mickey was greeted by his youngest son, Sam, who had the morning's recalcitrant pup in his arms.

'What are you doing, squirt?' Mickey said.

'Mum had to drop me off. She had to take Luke to his drama class. She reckons I'm a bastard just like you. She said we deserved each other. She's going to ring you about me staying a few days.'

'Mum's not too good then?' Mickey asked, walking on, looking down at Sam and the pup. 'How do you like the little tike?'

'He's terrific.' The pup was squirming round in his arms trying to get down to the ground, but then it relaxed again. 'Mum's good too. You don't hate her or anything, do you?'

'Of course I don't hate her. Whatever gave you that idea?' Georgia looked at Mickey with raised eyebrows as she walked past.

'Luke said. He still cries a bit. There's this club of kids at school, who've all got no father. They said we could join.'

'What are you talking about? You've got a father. Me. Don't you ever forget that. Hey, do you want to take that little bloke home?'

'Could I?'

'Yeah, so long as it's all right with Mum. And if somebody claims him, and they might, they get him back, right?'

Sam walked to the car and let the pup lick his face while Mickey opened the door. He slid over on the front seat and the pup jumped onto the back seat and immediately pissed on it. Sam looked up at Mickey, but Mickey was talking to Georgia. Georgia gave him

110

a wave. He didn't wave back; he was watching Mickey.

'I'll see you later tonight?' Mickey asked.

'Mmm, maybe,' Georgia said. 'I'll give you a ring. You'll probably need time with Sam, remember. I take it you've got some stuff to sort out with him. I'd be in the way.'

'Dad, the pup has pissed on the seat.'

Mickey came back to the car, opened the boot, took out a rag and tossed it into Sam. 'If you have a pup, you have to do everything, right?'

As she made her way back through the garage to pick up her stuff from the locker rooms she ran into Gina. They'd had little time to get together lately. They had smiled at each other sympathetically, each thinking: well, I'd like to talk, but they had simply not got around to anything more than their quick-witted banter. Gina had a large bag with her and Georgia imagined she was probably off to a singing gig.

'You won't need a job around here soon,' Georgia said lightly. 'Do you sing every night?'

'It's mainly Wednesdays to Saturdays.'

Georgia could see Gina's appeal. There was a firmness of eye and an openness about her expression that said, you can ask me anything you like and you'll get a straight response.

'It was a surprise for everyone,' Georgia said. 'You and Ridgy.'

'Not to me,' Gina said. She smiled at Georgia.

'Mickey and Angel were bitterly disappointed.' I'm really rushing things here, Georgia speculated. But it was also a way of cutting through the bullshit. Acknowledging that Gina was very attractive; perhaps a lot more.

'Hey, it's like I told you before. I can't just take—you know. It's not like that. Ridgy appealed to me immediately. He had something about him that was wise, that made me think he wouldn't be into the usual sort of judgements that men have. Younger blokes anyway. I'm not so sure that he is like that though.'

'Oh, do you want to talk about it? Can I give you a lift anywhere?' Georgia asked.

'No, it's all right. But thanks, and the band is picking me up. We're eating first.'

'We'll have to have lunch or something soon,' Georgia said.

'Sure,' Gina said. 'I'd like that.'

As Georgia went up the stairs a van pulled up and Gina waved and jumped into the side door. That was where the difference between Mickey and Ridgy lay. A relationship with Mickey wouldn't have allowed her to leave the depot with four or five young blokes in a van, band or not.

* * *

Ridgy drove down to the Crows Nest pub where Gina was singing. He entered the crowded bar where the topless barmaids were serving the patrons. They were strangely unappealing, they were doing a job, nothing more. He wondered how they felt about their bodies.

Gina was terrific as she alternately breathed husky words and bounced orgasmic cries over the audience. There was a driving beat to the music which Ridgy was less able to ignore than on the last occasion he heard the music.

Now it lifted away from him that feeling of being left behind. Not that the awareness of that wouldn't return. But the squad was changing. The Wilson and Prosser stuff had certainly altered things. He supposed he would have to make a decision now on which way to jump. Earlier, he would have been prepared to just go along with the status quo. Well, now that status quo was shifting. He didn't understand the rest of the squad's concern for the environment. He was a city boy and didn't feel at home out beyond the end of the suburban railway lines. They could pour concrete over everything as far as he was concerned. Not that he didn't love the sea, and he even agreed it was a pity they were pouring untreated shit into it, even if it was a kilometre off the beaches.

He knew he didn't have Gina's measure either. He'd never travelled beyond the image of woman as a person who found her identity only through a man. This one was way out ahead of him, prepared to resign over a relationship she had created but which was now a burden. He wanted to talk to her, to alleviate the pain of the abruptness of what was happening, but he wasn't sure he was going to avoid the pain. Would he have to go back to being happy having a few beers with Mickey or Sootie? Jesus!

Gina finished her song and came over to him. 'Hi,' she said. 'I'm glad you came. You were working late tonight?'

'Yeah, we were up on that river valley, beautiful spot.'

'I thought you rescued people.'

'Yeah, so did I.'

'Look, Ridgy, I can't go home with you tonight.'

'Yeah,' Ridgy said. 'Why?'

'Because I'm different from you. I thought you knew what I was about. I don't like young blokes because they stake you out as theirs, you know. I don't like that. Now I think that's what you'd like to do too; maybe it's inevitable, but I'm going to fight it.'

'It, what's it?'

'The game, Ridgy.'

'Yeah, I suppose so.' He was wondering whether he could fake being a different person. Pretend that he wasn't an old romantic fool. He doubted he could flesh out the new sort of bloke, though. Actually, the way he saw it, the new sort of bloke had been around for a while. He was the one who didn't care too much about anything. It was his turn now to be a winner. The problem was the new bloke wouldn't be satisfied by the win. It would just be another part of the game to him. Was that the new sort of life for everyone? It would certainly be easier. Perhaps the whole bloody world would be better off without passion. He shook his head, recognising that his need to possess her was wrong. Already it was making him bitter.

'Got time for a drink?'

'Sure.' Gina said. At least he could bask in the envy of the others at the bar. Perhaps there would even be some new blokes there with covetous eyes.

'By the way,' Ridgy said. 'Did Adams ask you to take stuff off the hard disc the other day?'

'Yes, he did. Why?'

'Were they specific items?'

'Yes. Why?'

'What were they?'

'Hey, is this stuff serious, or what?'

'Could be.'

'Well, he said to take out anything that wasn't staff, administration, or basic data.'

Ridgy realised then just how cunning the old bastard was. Maybe he didn't know computers but he knew how to order them around.

'Did you look at the things that came off?'

'No, I've been working through most of the documents there. There isn't much really. I knew straight away the documents that were to go.'

'Did he ask you to make a list of those documents?'

'No, but I saved them all on disc anyway. People ask you to clear stuff off the hard disc and then crack up when it's gone. You know, tear their hair. I always save a copy of the stuff now.'

Ridgy was relieved. He laughed and grabbed her hand. 'Hey, you're terrific,' he said.

'Why?' she asked. He just smiled at her. He wasn't going to tell her why. He had harboured a vague suspicion that everything had been a complete set up. She had come aboard just about the time Special Operations would have been planning the raid. If it had been a set up they would have needed someone in the depot—although it seemed that in Adams they had one anyway. It was a great relief to his vanity that this woman had chosen to care for him, no matter what the reason. It made him part of the human race again. He had begun to regard himself as little more than a function. But all the same, he was glad to hear the clear sincerity of her responses. She wasn't a Special Ops plant.

Meanwhile, his response had piqued Gina's curiosity.

115

'You do care about your job, don't you? I mean seriously. You probably care more about it than you cared about me.'

'Probably,' he said.

He was rewarded for not caring too much about her, by being permitted to take her home. The world is going crazy, he thought. Maybe she wouldn't be leaving the squad after all.

There was a certain piquancy to their love-making, each thinking that it may well be the last time with each other. Ridgy would always think it was the last time every time. He was a pessimist whose secret to life was that he was constantly surprised by how good life could be.

Around three in the morning he got out of bed to look out into the Sydney night.

He was always reassured by this city. If criminals made it run, too bad; there was not much he could do about it. Mickey was always hot down the trail of something that would make him angry, feel alive. Was that it for Mickey? Or was his anger real? Did he really want to change things? Of all of them, it was probably only Georgia who had the capacity to change anything. He wasn't sure how she would go about it, but it wouldn't be in the Rescue squad. She was learning here; discovering how things really were.

If she looked after her ambitions, kept her ideas to herself, didn't bleed about them around the squad or in bars, she might, in a decade or two, be in a situation where she could make a difference. The problem would be that she'd need a lot of mates to help her out.

He turned back from the window and looked at

Gina in the moonlight. Ridgy knew he was about to either miss the mid-life crisis or be bowled over by it. The catalyst either way would be this young woman in his bed.

He had nothing in common with her, although maybe there was some liking for honesty that they shared. She was certainly straight in personal relationships, and he knew he was honest with himself, if not always completely honest with others. Honesty needs good timing, he speculated. The truth has its own way of showing it has to be told. Which brought him to the raceday raid. What the hell could anyone do about it? Mickey was trumpeting away as if something could be done. He reasoned that Mickey was able to be so confident about the big things because every day on the road he successfully solved problems that others couldn't even begin to get their brains around. The problem with Mickey was that he never really knew just how big things were, and had no patience with the strategy of learning.

What could he do though? He could give a disc to the press, but they wouldn't use it unless it could be verified, unless he was prepared to stand up and be counted. Even then, they might not release it. And even if they did, the revelations would be limited, for by law there was no defence against defamation and libel in New South Wales. That was a dirty little out, to help save those who ran the state.

He had to admit one thing though. He felt better that people like Mickey and Georgia were around. They were solid stuff. He stood at the window for a time savouring the friendship he had with those two, until Gina moved in the bed and he craved the warmth of her. He slipped back between the sheets and attempted to caress her to further intimacy, but she took his hand and placed it firmly on her hip. 'Hey,' she mumbled, 'are you some sort of sex maniac?' Ridgy lay back, smiling to himself. Her accusation made him feel pretty good.

* * *

Out in the Wallagarra Valley the night was marvellous. The forest was bathed in the hot croaking of frogs. It sounded as if thousands of them were pulsing their throats in simultaneous waves, punctuated by higher or lower calls of hundreds of others of different species. Such a symphony as that had to produce friction in the night sky, had to produce a tangible heat. Above them the stars moved the heavens. Away from the reflections of the city the night sky was clear for their light show.

It was nights such as these that enabled Jacqui Napier to continue protesting. Nights in the wilderness were something else. Until she had begun camping, sleeping out, she hadn't believed the enthusiasm of her friends. Of course it helped that the nights were warm. There was nothing more miserable than wind and rain blasting through your tent.

During the day Jacqui had chosen her tree, a huge old gum with a healthy shining foliage. It would be one of the next to fall to the bulldozers. Now she was walking to it through the forest, just above the new road, with her friends Tod and Ian. They didn't want her to do this, but her mind was set on it. Up until now in the protests she hadn't asserted herself in any way at all. She couldn't bring herself to lie in front of

118

bulldozers. However, she thought she could bring herself to overcome her dislike of heights and stay in the tree platform that Tod and Ian had erected close to the top of the old gum.

The two boys had constructed tree houses before on other sites. They were dedicated to saving the forests, and had survival skills equal to any special military forces—except for firearms. They were quick and sure, she knew. There was nothing that they didn't consider in their construction. No nails. Everything was bolted, twice. The platform was covered by canvas, lashed to the structure, and they would send her up food and water when she lowered a rope. In the same way, she could send down waste. They had already placed enough food on the platform for a forty-eight hour squat up there.

Tod leaned against the tree, holding the rope ladder. He looked at her keenly. 'It should be all right Jacqui, but I'm not guaranteeing it. Are you sure you want to do this?'

She looked at him with a serious gaze. 'It's the only way,' she said, although she didn't feel confident about the climb.

'Yeah, but if you're at all worried, you know, I could do it. Or Ian.'

'No, this is something I *can* do. I know I can.'

'You're all by yourself up there,' Tod said, looking up.

A beam of light splashed through the forest at the same time that they heard the whine of a four-wheel drive motor. 'The bastards are here again,' Ian said. 'If you're going, go now.'

The two boys held the rope ladder steady and firm

with their weight and Jacqui started to climb. Don't look down, she told herself, don't look down.

No matter how much weight the boys put on the bottom of the rope it didn't stop it from swaying, wobbling even, in the middle heights. I just have to hold on, she told herself, and take one step at a time. It'll soon be over. If I was closer to the ground I wouldn't worry about my hold a bit. She stopped once to look closely at the tree trunk. In the starlight it was a marvellous thing, smooth, a gleam of sap, a strip of bark hiding insects, a gentle movement. It was a symbol of something, she wasn't sure what. This was one tree that wouldn't hit the ground, except in its own time.

Nine

The moment Mickey arrived at work he knew it was on again at the valley. Georgia and Angel were packing extra climbing ropes, and Frog was carrying two chainsaws.

'Are we supposed to be helping with the cutting and clearing now?' Georgia asked, sardonically. 'There's no way I'm touching one of those bloody things,' she added, indicating the chainsaws.

Adams heard the comment and poked his head over the stairwell. 'One of those bloody protesters, a girl too, is up one of the trees, about fifty metres up. We've got to bring her down.'

Mickey and Georgia had done a little research the night before. The protesters were attempting to save not only the forest from the highway, but also the coast: they were certain that a rumoured development on the small bay beach would go ahead—with bodgy environmental impact studies. In Australia the governments of both persuasions scarcely bothered to pretend that environmental impact studies were anything but bodgy. They were carried out by companies that had interests in developing an area. How bodgy could you get? Sure they employed 'independent' research companies. But these knew that a report that meant no development for one company meant no work from any other companies wanting to expand or develop. As Georgia well knew, after overhearing Lloyd Prosser and Burke, the bay development *would* go ahead. All that would be needed later was a branch road off this one that they were pushing through the forest.

Mickey and Georgia were certainly not going to be a great deal of help this morning on the protest site. They had decided they would not cut people free of the dozers, and they would not cart people to the vans. Their squad had been formed to rescue people. They were not going to be instruments of a corrupt administration. The decision to open up the forest and the bay had been made under the influence of bribes. They knew that. It seemed everyone did, but still there was a reluctance by the people who knew to act decisively. The forest was hours out of the city; camping there was uncomfortable; there was the awkwardness of defying authority, especially if it was paying your wage; and finally there was the likelihood that the government would ignore the results of any consultative procedures anyway.

The squad arrived at the valley in time to hear Burke talking to the press at the base of Jacqui's tree. Protesters were thin on the ground. Hundreds had been arrested, and weekdays saw most back at their jobs. Georgia looked up to the tree house. She could see the top of the girl's head. Jacqui was obviously sitting down, but although she appeared to be trying to hear what was going on below, she was not leaning over to find out. 'She's scared of heights,' Georgia said to Mickey.

'Yeah,' he said.

Press secretary Burke was explaining to the assembled media the procedures that had been available to the protesters.

'We heard their views in the committee hearings,' Burke was saying as news cameras rolled. 'The government has bent over backwards to accommodate them, and now they're into cheap stunts.'

Georgia felt like asking, how had they tried to accommodate them? Perhaps the media questions would come later.

'They are vandals and hooligans,' Burke continued. Georgia wanted to say, look around at this scar through virgin forest and then tell me who are the vandals?

Burke paused, perhaps expecting a question. 'These people are hooligans. I mean let's get some intelligence into this debate. Do you really think they're serious about the environment? They're only serious about getting their faces on television. I thought we would have grown beyond this type of stupid behaviour, frankly.'

Mickey nudged Georgia. 'If she struggled up there, it would be very dangerous for her . . . and us.'

A reporter jumped in as Burke paused again. 'What about the latest opinion polls?'

'What opinion polls?' Burke asked.

'The ones in *Forest Network* that show the public is against the road. That makes you the vandals, as far as the community is concerned.'

'Come off it. A few magazines phoning a few people does not constitute an opinion poll. They were underground magazines at that. Half of them

123

are printed on a photostat machine.'

Georgia looked at Mickey. 'No-one else would do a poll like that.'

Burke was not fazed. 'All our research has shown strong community backing for the whole project.'

'What research is that?' a woman's voice asked. Georgia turned to look at the reporter. The woman had that direct, bold look that accompanies someone who has met most challenges in their life, and hasn't been too depleted by the failures.

Burke side-stepped the question. 'Look,' he said angrily, 'these people have got to realise they are holding up progress, commitments. People's jobs are at stake here. The government has an agreement with the developers, and we are not about to back out now. That's it. That's all I've got to say.'

Georgia was dumbfounded that the press were silent. Did they still believe that anger stemmed from sincerity? Were they going to allow him to leave without further questions? She walked over to the woman who had interjected. 'How do you let him get away with it?'

'He won't,' the woman answered. 'Not in my story. I'm with the *Independent Weekly*, and we do it a little differently than the rest. Tell me, are you against the road?'

'Yes,' said Georgia.

'And you're part of the process of moving the protesters?'

'No, not any more. I'm from Police Rescue and we're only here to see no-one is hurt.'

'So the police are divided on this one?' the woman

asked. She looked at Georgia deeply, searching her eyes.

'No more than the community,' Georgia said. 'We're all human.'

'Aah yes, but we're led to believe that you're conditioned to obey.' The woman was ironic now, smiling.

'No, there are some attitudes in the force that have developed because of the work they have to do. But in Rescue we're really only helping people. Like helping that girl out of the tree if she wants or needs help.'

Georgia saw Mickey and Angel bringing the ropes from the truck. 'Sorry, I've got to go,' she said. 'Work.'

'I'll talk to you later,' the woman said. 'I'm Cassandra Douglas.'

Mickey was talking to the sergeant when she walked up. 'She got any food or water?'

'Her mate said she had enough to last until tomorrow. Then they're sending up more. How you gonna get her?'

'No idea, mate.'

Burke came up to join the group. 'Hi, good to see you. Darryl Burke.' He proffered his hand, but Mickey had his full of ropes and he wasn't going to drop them. He didn't return the salutation, either.

'You the bloke who called us in?'

'Me? No, we got the Minister to speak to someone at headquarters and he's not too happy I can tell you. I've got to try and keep this lot off him.' Burke laughed for no particular reason. 'Go and get her will you. I'll be damned glad when this is over. Oops. Here's trouble,' he said, as two reporters approached. 'They'll want to know how you're going to do it. Don't worry, I'll handle them.'

'Don't talk for me,' Mickey said. Burke stopped and looked at Mickey. His eyes were flat: so you don't take bullshit? I'll remember you. Mickey shrugged at him: that's the way it is. Already they were firm enemies.

Angel had tossed a rope over a pretty high branch on the other side of the tree, about ten metres up. 'This rope is safe I reckon, Mickey,' he said, leaning his weight on it.

'It better be,' Mickey said. 'The last time I went up a tree this high I was eleven, and I fell out of it.'

'So that's the reason,' Angel said.

Mickey gave him a quizzical look. Angel wound his finger at the side of his head. 'Get stuffed,' Mickey said.

Mickey took the rope from Angel and attached his harness to it.

'How's she going to get down?' Angel asked.

'The same way she went up,' Mickey answered, beginning to climb.

'She won't just come down,' the sergeant said to Sootie, who had come to see how the land lay.

'Mate, that bloke's talked down more jumpers than you've had hot dinners.'

'Yeah, but she's not a jumper.'

'Same sort of person though,' Sootie said. 'Same mental equipment.' The sergeant turned away, shaking his head at Sootie's ignorance.

Mickey looked out over the forest a few times as he

made his methodical climb. Lucky it wasn't an old red gum, their branches often fell without warning. Not even a sound until they were on their way. The river was a sparkling silver ribbon in the morning sun. He'd bring his kids out here.

He saw Jacqui look over the edge of the platform when he was about six metres off.

'G'day,' Mickey said.

'Police Rescue?' Jacqui said, reading the words on his overalls. 'They should have told you. I don't need rescuing.'

'Yeah, they did. Just thought I'd come up and check it out myself.'

Mickey reached the platform and hauled himself aboard in the style of slipping out of a swimming pool.

'I'm not going down.'

'Fair enough, what's your name?'

'What's yours,' Jacqui demanded aggressively.

'Mickey.'

'You don't look like a Mickey.'

'So what's your name?'

'I told you, I'm not going down.'

Mickey fastened his rope to the trunk of the tree. Somebody would have to come up and untie it. Angel could do that.

'OK, let's cut it out,' he said. 'I can help you down.' He smiled at her as if he were indulging a small child. 'You're causing a lot of inconvenience.'

'That's the general idea.' Mickey revised his opinion of her and searched for another way. Perhaps she was going to last the distance, focus public opinion. He wanted to be sure though, before he left her there.

127

Play the game right the way through.

She was a slim girl, and reasonably attractive. She would be unrecognisable from a million others like her in the street. But she was displaying steel that came from an understanding of how things worked here in the forest, and an anger at the destruction of something she loved and believed in.

Her look was a bit too comfortable though, as though she had been sheltered too long. Sort of middle class. He put this last doubt to the test. He wasn't going to encourage someone who couldn't play their part.

'Now listen to me. Your photo is gonna be in all the papers. Your daddy will see you on television tonight. He'll be really proud of his little girl. You'll be famous. But don't push it. I could take you down very easily, even if you resist.'

'My father died two years ago.'

'Sorry.'

'It's all right. I don't really think about him that much anyway.'

'You will though,' Mickey said, rising to his feet. 'Now I can get you out of this two ways.'

'Are you arresting me?'

Mickey squatted again. Most people who asked that question were frightened. She was perfectly matter-of-fact.

'Yeah, I could.'

'OK, so I'm arrested. How do you get me down, knock me out?'

Mickey shook his head and then looked out over the valley from the tree house. 'Lovely spot you've got here.'

'Isn't it wonderful.'

Mickey rose again. The tree swayed a little, the platform creaked. 'Sit down, sit down, please,' she said.

'Hey, take it easy, it's all right.'

'Sorry, you scared me. Everything seemed to move at once.'

'You're scared of height, right? My partner said you were.'

'Terrified sometimes.'

'Then why are you up here?'

'It's important.'

'It's dangerous for you, being up here when you're scared. If you get nausea or vertigo at the wrong time, you'll freeze up. You'd be a real mess if you fell.'

'I'll be right.'

'It's just a road, you know. You'd risk your life for a road?'

'Not only the road. That's the whole point. Why do they want to put a road through here in the first place? Where's it going to go to that can't be reached by another road?'

'You're going after some pretty tough blokes.' Was he being patronising? He couldn't help himself.

'I know, but if this road goes ahead, all of this, the last stretch of forest between the bay and the city will disappear.'

Mickey tapped the platform with his fingers, emphasising beforehand the point he was going to make. 'These blokes are tough. They don't muck around. If they follow the precedents laid down by some other developers in the city they could even kill you.'

'I know.' Mickey saw that she did know, that she

had geared herself for anything. He liked her a lot. 'OK, you stay here.' He took the rope and began lowering himself over the side.

'Don't fall,' she said.

'Hope not.'

Even before he got to the ground he could hear Burke's voice complaining. 'What are you doing? Where is she? Are you leaving her up there?'

'Why don't you pipe down?' Mickey said, landing beside him. 'You're a real blowhard aren't you?'

Burke looked at him, remembered their previous exchange, and spoke in a whisper. 'Let's go and talk over there for a tic.'

Mickey winked at Georgia, and followed Burke to another tree ten metres away.

'What the hell is going on here, Sergeant? I want the girl down now. The government wants the girl down now.'

'Well, you know,' Mickey said. 'That same government tells me to save lives, not risk them, do you understand? Do you think I'm just a servant for your developer mates? That I'd risk the girl's life for them?'

'I see,' Burke said turning away, looking at the ground, doing a poor imitation of thinking.

'That Wallagarra Bay development that was supposed to be pigeon-holed, is it going ahead then?'

Burke turned back, thinking there was sympathy here he could work on. 'Of course it is, that's the reason we want all this fixed up. We announce it this week.' He stopped when he saw he wasn't talking to a sympathiser.

'Yeah, I knew it was,' Mickey said. 'I just wanted you to know that everyone knows what's going down here; that you're not fooling anyone. Except yourself that is. You've got to ask yourself who are the vandals now, mate.'

Mickey began walking back. 'Listen,' Burke called out. 'She's in the way, Sergeant. If you don't do as you're told, you'll be reported.'

'Listen, you stuck pig, I don't take orders from anyone but my superiors, right? Now in matters like this, where a life is at risk, they take my word on it.

'I'm leaving her there. She's not in any physical danger, but she might have been if we tried to drag her down. We'll keep an eye on her.'

Mickey walked with Angel to the van. Georgia signalled to Jacqui to pull the rope up and, lurking near the tree where Burke stood with his mobile phone, she managed to overhear his conversation.

'Yeah, gloves are off. We'll have to isolate her. And you can organise getting her down.' He turned to the nearby police officer. 'Sergeant, we need to quarantine her. Do you need something official to do that?'

'We can keep the area clear now,' the sergeant said, obeying his political masters. 'But after tomorrow, I'll have to have something from headquarters.'

'Yeah, that's right,' Burke laughed into the phone, a strange laugh that had nothing to do with humour. 'It'll have to come down officially, so tell him to fix it. We want every last one of them in the slammer. Yeah, right, bye.'

Georgia walked back to the group. 'These kids don't know what they're up against,' she said. 'They're organising something pretty nasty.'

Back at the depot, Ridgy confronted Mickey. 'You left her up there?' he asked.

'There was no rescue involved. She wants to stay up there. She's perfectly safe.'

Ridgy had sympathy with Mickey's position, but he wasn't going to indulge him. Mickey had to make these sorts of decisions all by himself. It was up to him to discover how far he wanted to go. 'Think about it Mickey. Don't defy everyone without having a position.'

Ptomaine, the Rescue squad kitchen hand, often had really bright ideas. 'You could do it, Ridgy. Go up there and just grab her as if she was a jumper.'

'She's not a jumper,' Mickey said. 'She's sane, she's smart, and she hates being up there.'

'So what's she doing it for?'

'Ptomaine, she's a protester. She believes it's important, right?'

Ridgy rubbed the sole of his boot along the floor. 'It'll be Special Operations that gets her down,' Ridgy advised. 'It won't be pleasant for her.'

Mickey recognised the comment as a ruse. 'They'll be in trouble if they do. You can tell them from me any rough stuff and she'll go off the tree, and they'll have a martyr on their hands. They will have earned the undying bloody hatred of everyone, if they haven't already.'

'Aah, come off it, Mick. This is not you talking. These aren't your words.'

'Ridgy, it's not what we're about. This public servant rings the Minister for Development and Finance, he rings our headquarters. I mean who the hell are we rescuing here?'

'The government,' Angel said.

'Exactly,' Mickey confirmed.

132

'Yeah Ridgy,' Frog added, 'if the government's got a problem, it's not our job to fix it.'

'We're talking of freedom of speech, really, Ridgy,' Georgia said. 'The government's trying to hide the development on the bay, the real reason for the road. It's going to be a fait accompli. No discussion, nothing. At least in Victoria they have a huge debate to find out the mood of an electorate and then steamroller them. That way they know where everyone stands. The hypocrisy is upfront, and the people vote them out. Here they control the media, everything.'

'This is gonna cause real trouble, Mick.'

'Hey, Ridgy, doesn't releasing Vic Wilson cause trouble?' Mickey said. 'We all know what he's doing. We all know what Prosser's been up to. Damn it, Travis from Special Ops said that raid would get Prosser. So they have him and they let him go.'

Adams came to the door of the canteen. 'How do you know what they have Mickey?' he asked.

'Because I watched Georgia putting the files on your hard disc, remember?'

Adams shook his head. 'Yeah, pity we can't check it now. I doubt our Ministers of the Crown would want to go along with a crook.'

'You've got to be kidding,' Mickey said.

'No I'm not kidding, Mickey. It's called sarcasm,' Adams said. 'I'm just making sure the squad is minding its own business.'

'Crime isn't police force business?' Mickey asked.

'Yeah, and so is doing what it's told,' Adams said. 'Now, if you, a sergeant, know better than our bosses how we should act, I suggest you apply for a super's job.'

'I didn't know we had to ask permission to go after the bad guys,' Mick said.

'We don't, but we are split into various parts, and you don't decide which parts do what. That's the job of others. They get paid for deciding what goes on.'

'Yeah,' Mickey said. 'But what if they're bent?'

'Discovering that is not your job either, Mickey.' Adams pulled himself up to his full height, an exercise he wasn't used to. 'This squad does what I tell them, right? We don't catch crooks, beyond the ones that fall into our laps, and we don't decide police policy.'

'We should have some input,' Georgia said. 'When we suspect something is wrong we should report it. We ask the public to do it every day.'

Adams shook his head and turned back to his office. 'I can see there's going to be some changes around here,' he threatened. Georgia knew it was directed at her. The men had nothing to worry about. Not even Mickey, Adams valued him too highly.

Ten

Some days later Mickey and Sam were playing with the pup during the late news. The pup was full of itself. 'He must have been boss of the litter,' Mickey said. It pounced around on the paper that littered the floor, wagged its tail and lolled its tongue. It was a smart little bugger. The three of them were laughing.

The newsreader read the Wallagarra Valley item over shots of the magnificent scenery. Mickey looked at the television as Sam and the pup rolled over each other, the pup trying to lick Sam's face. 'The hunger strike by protester, Jacqueline Napier, went into its second day today, amid claims that the government had earlier prevented any food being sent to her. Protest leaders . . .'

Sam was not interested in the news. 'Will we really have to give him back, Dad? Why Dad?'

'Ssssh,' Mickey sounded. 'I'm listening.'

The news reporter was standing now in front of the tree as the camera panned upwards. '. . . in the last three days in a tree house in a bid to stop the controversial development . . .'

'But why can't I keep him?'

'Just a minute,' Mickey said impatiently.

Burke's big face filled the screen. 'That is absolute

nonsense. No-one is depriving her of food. It was her decision to go on this hunger strike. We have spent the last two days trying to get food up to her, and she's refusing it.'

Jacqui's friend Tod replaced Burke on the screen. 'No, she didn't originally plan it as a hunger strike, but, ah, now she's been forced into it, she's totally serious, and we're backing her all the way.'

Mickey commented aloud, 'She's got some guts.'

'But,' said Sam, 'they left him all by himself.'

Mickey shook his head in resignation. 'I told you that was the other bloke. When the owners come back you'll have to hand him over. Hey, and you haven't eaten anything.'

'I'm not hungry,' Sam said.

'Come on, you're not eating because you can't keep the pup.'

'I don't want it. I feel sick.'

The doorbell rang and Mickey left the living room and walked down the hall to the door. He wasn't sure who to expect. Georgia was smiling at him.

'Georgia!' Mickey exclaimed.

'Who were you expecting, Madonna?'

To let everyone know how things stood he called, 'Sam, Georgia's here.'

'I thought he'd be asleep by now,' Georgia said in a whisper.

'The pup, you know.'

'I'll go.'

'No, no come in.'

'You sure?'

Georgia walked into the living room. 'G'day Sam.'

'Do you live here with dad?'

'No. But I visit him sometimes.'

'Those your ear rings in the bathroom?'

'I hope so,' Georgia said under her breath.

'All right, Sam,' Mickey said, 'it's time for bed. Georgia and I have to talk about work.'

Mickey propelled Sam towards the bedroom, the pup in his arms. 'I've got a name for him,' Sam said.

'No, no names, Sam, we agreed on that. You'll only think he's yours then.'

Tucked into bed, the pup set to keep him awake for half the night, Sam asked Mickey if he loved Georgia.

'I love you, Sam, and Luke, you know that.'

'What about Mum?'

'We do love each other in a sort of a way. We're just . . . separate.'

'Why?'

'I don't know, son. It's a hard question. It just happens sometimes. Don't you worry, you'll be all right.'

'I'm worried about Mum.'

'Why?'

'Well, she should have someone too.'

'Yeah, sure, Sam. She will. You wait and see. Goodnight.' Mickey rose and turned off the light.

Out in the living room Georgia asked what he thought could be done about the girl in the Wallagarra Valley.

'Not much. We've left her there. She has friends on the ground.'

'But what can we do?'

'Not much else.'

'But we know who's behind this. We know what they're doing.'

'So? I have no idea what we can do.' He hated saying he couldn't do anything, but he had to be frank with her. 'Georgia, I've really tried to think through this. I'm lost on this one.'

'We could go the press.'

'Give them the information on the disc you mean?'

'What else?'

'We would have to reveal ourselves, place ourselves in danger. Nothing would happen immediately anyway. They would have the stuff with lawyers for months.'

'Yeah, but something would be in the pipeline. It would be moving ahead.'

'I'm not good at that sort of stuff. I need it to happen and be over with. I hate being locked into things, and finding out new things all the time that throw you.'

'You're good at all that when you're on a rescue, it's no different.'

'Yeah, but I know I'm doing the right thing, and it's over at the end of the day. I know I'm not going to have to think about it every day for years wondering if I want out or not. I'd get sick of it.' He looked at her and took her hand. 'I'd be scared I'd just give in to all the shit they piled on top of me.'

In the morning they dropped Sam off at school before heading for the depot. 'See you, mate,' Mickey said.

'Yeah, Dad,' Sam said, his voice bordering on truculence.

Ridgy came on the blower when they were only minutes away. Mickey told him where they were, and Ridgy said he'd meet them in the garage. 'Looks interesting,' Mickey said.

'Yeah,' Georgia said. 'I'm looking forward to it.'

Ridgy walked up to the driver's side of the vehicle as soon as it stopped.

'What's doin'?' Mickey asked, deliberately casual.

'The shit's hit the fan, Mickey.'

'What sort of shit?'

'The kid up the tree in the valley; well, the government are looking for someone to blame.'

'Yeah?'

'Well, they chose us. That Burke fellow is serving us up.'

'That ferret.'

'The government's looking bad, now, and they're after your blood.'

'The boss was up there most of yesterday, keeping the dogs off you. But he can't hold out too much longer. He's told them you're going there this afternoon to get her down.'

Mickey lowered his voice to reply. 'What do you reckon, Ridgy? You know what's going down out there? The government's leading every one of us by the nose. I happen to like that wilderness area, and the government is going to stuff up that bay without even telling anyone they've made the decision.

'They're flying in the face of public opinion, and for who? The blokes we could've arrested after the raid. They had all the dirt on them they needed, thanks to Georgia.'

'It's up to you, Mickey. I can't go along with planned disobedience.'

'We're supposed to serve the public, Ridgy.'

Ridgy whispered this time. 'We're talking about dangerous blokes here. Now I'm sending you out. Adams would explode if he saw you now.'

'Mightn't be a bad idea,' Georgia said.

* * *

Georgia and Mickey still had no plan by the time they reached the valley. As Georgia put it, there were too many variables, too many changing circumstances. They could only act if there was an opportunity to act. 'The timing has to be right or we're going to look like a bunch of green cops who are only sounding off. And we can't release a lot of the stuff,' she concluded, 'because of the libel laws in this bloody state.'

The tree had become a focus for the media. Georgia saw all the fresh moss and fungi around the roots had been trampled.

Interminable television reports were still being filmed, despite the fact that there were more press than protesters. No doubt footage from earlier days would be cut in at the news room. As Mickey prepared to climb, another Rescue van arrived. Angel and Frog climbed out.

'We're here to see you do it right,' Frog said.

'Who sent you?' Mickey asked. 'Adams and Ridgy?'

'He's going up with you,' Frog said, gesturing towards Angel.

All around them the press wanted to know the procedures for capturing the girl and dragging her down. Georgia looked for the *Independent Weekly* reporter. He was nowhere around.

A television reporter asked Mickey why he hadn't brought the girl down before. 'See, it's going to take two of you this time.' Georgia asked the reporter why he didn't report his personal views. 'If you're down on us for the job we do, why aren't you honest about yours?'

The reporter shrugged. 'It wouldn't be objective.'

'Then be objective about what we do.'

Mickey and Angel swarmed up the tree. At least that would look good on television.

Mickey looked up to see Jacqui watching them climb. When he reached the platform, he said, 'G'day.'

Angel was only a body length away and called out, 'Hi.'

'Hi,' Jacqui said.

'You know why we're here,' Mickey stated.

'Sure. Want a glass of water?' Jacqui asked. 'It's all I can offer you.'

'No, thanks,' Mickey said. 'Come on,' he added, more sympathetically. 'We'll help you down.'

'It's strange really, after a while you don't feel hungry, just a bit empty.'

'Jacqui,' Mickey said, earnestly. 'Come down now. In your state you could just about roll off here.'

'No,' Jacqui said.

'We could drag you off.'

'Of course you could.'

Then Angel tried his tactful best. 'Don't be stupid. You've got to come down.'

'You think I'm dumb doing this, don't you?'

'No,' Angel said. He and Mickey hauled themselves onto the platform. Their strength made it obvious that if they had wanted to they could have swept Jacqui up and taken her to the ground in seconds.

Jacqui waved her hand around the valley and through to the sea. 'Look, it's gorgeous isn't it? If this road goes through it'll be concrete and supermarkets and golf courses. And down on the bay will be a hotel for the rich people. Soon you'll have to travel two hours from the city to see any bushland. Who can afford to do that? The time or the money?'

'Jacqui, we're on you side,' Mickey said. 'There are other ways,' he added, recognising how lame it sounded.

'What other ways?' she asked, and began an explanation that was more directed to Angel than to Mickey. 'We went to all the committee hearings, and they wouldn't even listen. You could tell it was just a big set-up. They had an attitude they couldn't disguise. And you knew they were phoney because they all used the same demonstration kits. All of them had lessons in how to run over the opposition, and from the same people. They just lie to you, or leave out the key information. You can't trust any of them.

'We were going to demonstrate outside the developers' offices. And they invited us in and told us they weren't going ahead. They'd changed their minds. So we went home. The next day they put the proposals for the hotel and the road to the committee.

'I'm nineteen now, and already I can spot a bureaucrat who's lying, and I'm sick of it . . . sick of all those people. Now, I'm doing this. At least it's something honest.'

Mickey tried to coax her with his voice. 'But it's not

worth dying for—not a stretch of bushland. And dying is what we're talking about here. *Is* it worth dying for—this forest, the bay?' He was curious about her answer.

'You don't think so?' she asked. 'Then what do you die for?'

Mickey looked away, over the bushland, the river. 'I couldn't,' he said.

Angel looked at her, his lips parted in astonishment. He was seeing real courage here.

Jacqui looked over at Mickey squatting by the rail. 'I remember what you said the last time. I've been thinking a lot about my father.

'I wondered what he would think, about what I'm doing. You know what he'd say?'

'What?' Mickey knew his father wouldn't have been able to comprehend any of the things that were going on in the world. Since he had died it had been turned upside down. The whole agenda had changed now. For some it was the survival of the planet, for others a fight for the survival of progress and expansion. The battle lines were drawn.

'He'd say I'm crazy. He'd say I'm wrong. Maybe I am. One thing's for sure, they're not right.'

'Jacqui,' Mickey said softly. 'I'm leaving you here. But you've got to eat something. You've got to last so your protest lasts.'

Climbing down from the platform, Angel shook his head at Mickey. 'It's your job on the line, mate. But I agree with you.'

'I'll be wearing it,' Mickey said.

'I can cope with that,' Angel said, and there was laughter in his voice. Mickey looked up. Angel was

143

grinning down at him. At the bottom of the tree Mickey pushed past the press who had filmed his attempt, ignoring their facile questions. Let them make their own interpretation, he thought. They will anyway.

The drive back to the city was a drag. Mickey had been reinvigorated by the country air. Already he was thinking of camping trips with his sons.

'I'm sick of driving back all the time,' he said. 'They should put us up in a motel around here somewhere.'

'They'll be wondering how they can put you in a cell somewhere,' Georgia said.

The moment they drove in Adams came out from his office onto the steel scaffolding at the end of the garage. 'McClintock, get up here.'

Mickey ran up the stairs quickly, like a feisty show pony, his eyes moving up and down like Groucho Marx as they bounced off the team below. He followed Adams into his office.

Adams started right in. 'I've had it with you, McClintock. I've copped it sweet for you today. Now, just ten minutes ago I get a call from one of the Deputy Commissioners, asking why Rescue has *failed twice* to get a tiny girl out of that bloody tree.'

Mickey felt liberated. The powers of vengeance had been unleashed—and in the end it amounted to nothing. A demand to know. He could go further still and he wouldn't be troubled. He understood himself now, and that was worth giving away any number of promotions. So he wouldn't have a career? Did he really care? He didn't want one anyway. The work he was doing was the only work he loved. If he left the force he would find work as a ranger, a guide. Perhaps even his own survival business. He could see himself taking parties of women into the bush for lessons. He shook his head at his own gross fantasies. He brought his mind back to Adams. It was difficult.

'She was in no danger, Bill. Simple as that,' he answered.

'I don't give a damn what she's in ... danger or not. You were sent with four other officers to get her down. Why didn't you do it?'

'Well, you know, we risked our lives last Saturday and all the evidence was lost. Today you want me to risk someone else's life. Now, she wasn't doing anything. She was perfectly sane. There was no charge pending—at least, no-one told me to *arrest* her. Nothing. If she had struggled, she might have been hurt and then she would have sued. It would even have risked this squad. The public would have demanded to know what we were doing. The politicians would have caved in to the pressure, and they would have privatised us or something, right?'

'You bloody smart-arse. What sort of lip is this? You want to be a lone ranger, you go off and do it somewhere else. Got that?'

'Yes, sir.' Mickey said it smartly, obsequiously even, but Adams didn't catch the irony.

'You're facing a charge, Sergeant. There's likely to be more trouble over this. I'm not sitting here copping political heat because you're out there making some protest of your own.'

'Yes, sir.'

'From now on you fight your own fights, and not on Rescue time. And let me tell you you've got nothing to win with.'

Mickey nodded as if he thought that was the end of the interview and walked out the door, closing it carefully behind him.

Sam was in the canteen, talking to Ptomaine and looking worried. Behind him he heard Adams open the office door. 'You're off the job McClintock. You go within a mile of that bloody girl or her tree, and you're out of this squad. Got that?'

'Yes sir,' he said not turning around but winking at Sam.

'Someone else can bring her down. You're off active duty until you hear from me. See you later, Sergeant.'

Mickey walked into the canteen. 'How are you, Sam? Sootie pick you up all right?'

'Yeah. Are you getting the sack, Dad?'

'No, son.'

'Are you sure?'

Mickey winked at Sam in an easy way. He didn't want his son worried about this bureaucratic heaviness.

Ridgy walked over from the canteen queue. 'You're stupid, Mick. I told you what was going on.'

'For some strange reason, Ridgy, I find it difficult to arrest somebody who's not a criminal.'

'Yeah, but you've blown your career, mate. You'll be sitting doing public relations in primary schools for the next six months, if you're lucky.'

'They want her down for corrupt political reasons. Our job is not political.'

'You just made a political decision to leave her up

there,' Ridgy said. 'This time you're wrong mate.'

'Bullshit Ridgy,' Mickey said. 'Anyway, we know, don't we, that it's not really a political decision, it's a criminal one. Well, for the benefit of criminals. They're making a criminal decision; I'm making a political one.'

'Yeah, well think on this Mickey. You reckon she's in no danger up there; if she mysteriously falls out of that tree tonight, you'll last ten minutes.'

That night Mickey, Georgia and Sam ate at a Thai restaurant. The pup stayed at home. Sam was unusually quiet, although that was becoming a habit when Georgia was with his father. Knowing Sam's nature when he was upset, Mickey knew he couldn't talk to him while Georgia was with them. But to deceive him or lie to him about the nature of his relationship with Georgia was something he wasn't going to do. To talk about it too fully, too soon, was also going to be a problem. The timing would have to be right. As far as Mickey was concerned Sam had also to understand he could be good friends with people outside the family as well. And at the moment Mickey was too concerned with his own position in the world to give Sam much time at all.

Beneath their conversation, Mickey and Georgia were aware that they were opening up a huge void in their world. It looked as if they were going to have to descend into it, fighting dread all the way, or traverse it with trickery somehow. It was a temptation to drop the whole confrontational approach to it, and just revert to doing their 'duty' in the normal cold-blooded way. They knew though, that to do that would affect their whole approach to their job and to the people they worked alongside.

Mickey and Sam dropped Georgia off. 'I'll ring you,' Mickey said.

'Only if you've got a solution, or something to add,' Georgia said, 'because I'm hitting the sack right away. We've done all our talking. It's a matter of finding out what we can do.'

* * *

The next day Mickey was kept in at the depot, in case the Deputy Commissioner felt like taking him personally to task to relieve his anger. Georgia was at a fatal accident with Ridgy, and then on a body recovery from the harbour. Mickey spent his day cleaning up the vehicles, relaxing in the canteen with Ptomaine.

Around four o'clock Des called in to drop Sam off again. The pup jumped out of the car and looked up wagging its tail for Sam to emerge.

'Back again, Dad,' Sam said. He was obviously still delighted with the pup. So was Des.

'Great little pup,' she said to Mickey with heavy sarcasm. She took him aside. 'What the hell do you think you're doing? Sam loves that pup. He's going to be devastated when he has to give it back. You've got to think of his feelings Mickey. They're still a kid's feelings, and you treat him as if he's already a bloody man. I know how your father treated you, and we know that wasn't the way. Think of him, Mickey, not yourself. And can you tell your woman friend not to hang around all the time. It's got to be a slow process, understand?' Des spun away and walked back to the car. She waved and smiled at Sam and sped off.

Sam walked into the depot eating his hamburger. He broke some off to give to the pup.

'Stop that, Sam,' Mickey said.

'Why?' Sam's angry retort came too quickly.

'I don't know. You'll get germs or something.'

'No, I won't.' The words and tone were of open defiance.

'Yes you will, now stop it.'

'No.'

Mickey stopped and looked down at Sam. 'What's gone wrong? We were going great. What is it, Sam?'

Sam and the pup both looked up at Mickey. 'You just let your boss yell at you. You didn't say anything,' Sam said. Mickey could see Sam was on the verge of tears, but was keeping them at bay with his anger. 'You said you always have to stick up for yourself. If you're right, someone else can't make you wrong. You said.'

'But he was right.'

'Why?'

'Because he thought I'd done the wrong thing, and it's his job to get angry with me.'

'Were you wrong then?'

'Yes and no.'

'Why are you sticking up for that girl? You are aren't you?'

Mickey wondered why things got to be so complicated. He couldn't just say it was complicated though, and expect Sam to wear that. He had to tell him somehow. Where would he begin?

'You see, Sam, it *looks* as if she's breaking the law. She's trying to stop the road makers from going through the forest. She and her friends want to see the forest stay the same, they want to see the bay stay the same. She wants to save the wilderness forever so there are always birds, and animals and forests of trees. The government and the developers want to develop the area to make money. The forest will disappear and so will the birds and animals. Most of them anyway. Now I also believe it should stay the same, because there aren't very many wild areas left. Now if I believe the same thing she does, how can I arrest her?'

He didn't mention that the developers had criminal connections because that was getting too complicated. Anyway, it was irrelevant to the issue. A developer without criminal connections could have been involved.

Sam tousled the fur on the pup's head. 'How does *she* know what's right? How do *you* know what's right?'

'Well she convinced me, Sam.'

'What do you mean?'

'Well, there are some people that see things more clearly than the rest of us. They see how things are and they try and change it, even if it means breaking the law. And then finally, according to Georgia, the rest of us understand they were right. But by then it's too late, and we wish we had done something.'

'So why didn't you tell your boss when he was so mad at you?'

'Because he knows.'

Sam looked up from the pup. 'Well, that means everyone knows, don't they?'

Mickey sat down on the bumper of one of the vehicles. 'Yes they do, Sam. You're a very smart kid. And you know what? I'm very proud to be your dad.'

Mickey and Sam and Ptomaine were sitting in the

canteen. Frog was the first in after his job. 'God, what slackers,' he said to the trio. 'Hey, Mickey, there's a couple of blokes want to talk to you. I think I've seen them out at the valley. They're in the garage.'

Mickey walked down the steel stairs, watching the two men standing beside their motorcycle. He wasn't sure what to expect.

Tod, the taller of the two, stepped towards him. 'You're Sergeant McClintock, right.'

'Sure.'

'Jacqui mentioned you.'

'What can I do for you?' Mickey asked.

Tod indicated Angel, over to one side underneath the bonnet of the back-up vehicle.

'He's all right,' Mickey said.

'Jacqui's in trouble,' Tod said. 'There's nobody out there with her now but us, and these three guys came around this morning. They made a lot of threats.'

'What sort of threats?'

'That she's going to be found dead if we don't get her down quickly.'

'Tell me what sort of blokes they were.'

'Really heavy. I mean big. Nothing funny about them. Just dead pan, doing a job sort of thing.'

'Well what are you doing here? Tell the press. Tell the cops down there. Get out there now.'

'We've tried. The coppers there won't listen to us. We can't get near her. We can't trust the media, they've never told the real story. We're scared, this is really heavy.'

Angel stood up and slammed the bonnet down. 'Mick, the uniformed boys have sealed her off. Just let them handle it.'

'Oh yeah, you know how good they are. They'll be told to get out tonight, and they will.'

Angel rubbed the clamps he held with a piece of oily cloth. 'You know what's going to happen if you go anywhere near her, or the bloody tree.'

'I let her stay up there, now I'm going to get her down.'

'All right, I understand,' Angel said. 'I'm in.'

'Get Sootie,' Mickey said to Angel.

'He's off.'

'Yeah, well Georgia'll come.'

Angel was lightheaded with his decision. 'We're all going to get kicked out of the squad,' he said. The lightness in his heart was amazing to him.

Mickey arranged for Sam to go home with Sootie, and he and Georgia and Angel headed off in Georgia's car.

The first thing they noticed as the evening came down was that there was no activity at all. No police. No demonstrators. The huge red scar in front of Jacqui's tree was peaceful in the twilight.

Mickey jumped from the car. 'Jacqui, Jacqui,' he called. There was no answer. He wasn't sure if he saw movement or not. He turned back to Georgia. 'Get to the nearest phone and call headquarters. Get some uniformed cops back here fast. You two,' he said to Tod and Ian, 'get back up on the main road. If you see those blokes coming, you get back here and tell me.'

With Angel tossing the rope over the branches, Mickey scaled easily up the trunk.

'What's happening?' Jacqui asked. She seemed vaguer than when he had last seen her.

152

'Jacqui, listen to me. Listen hard. There are some men coming to get you out of the tree. They don't care how they do it. Do you understand?

'You could be found at the bottom, dead or alive. And you have no-one to protect you.'

'Who are they?' Jacqui asked. Mickey saw how she had hardened in her determination to such an extent she was probably beyond ordinary reason. His response would have to be shockingly convincing.

'They are people hired by the developers. They're not nice people at all. They'll hurt you. That's what they do.'

Georgia's car swung back into the clearing below them. Georgia sprang out calling, 'Mickey, there's a car coming up the dirt road from the bay.'

'That's them,' he said to Jacqui. 'Come on, let's go.'

'But you're a cop. I can't go. I promised myself.'

'Jacqui, they're in the killing business. They enjoy it. We'll be in the firing line as well. All the uniformed coppers have been withdrawn.'

'I don't understand.'

'Don't even try,' Mickey said. 'The fact is, we're all risking ourselves out here.'

'I've been risking myself. I'm not scared any more.'

Jesus, I'm no good at this stuff. Why isn't Georgia up here? Mickey thought. But he tried again. 'Listen, Jacqui, if you're going to die, you should die in your own way. Not the way someone else chooses.'

Georgia's voice came up softly from below. She had climbed the first third of the tree. 'Mick, they've stopped. They're coming up on foot.'

'OK, just watch them. Jacqui, you've got to come now.'

'But why are you worried? For yourself, I mean.'

He heard Georgia call something, but the voice came too quiet and he didn't hear.

He answered Jacqui. 'It wouldn't be the first time a copper has been shot in this state. By other coppers too.' His voice became desperate. 'I know you're battling these people the best way you know. I know that. But don't you see, if they end it here for you, they've won.'

'All right,' she said.

He attached a rope, hooked Jacqui into a harness, hooked the rope to his own, and took her down in an adapted abseil. Georgia was gone. He hoped she was with Angel, keeping out of trouble.

He half carried Jacqui in a run around the cleared red dirt to the main track. Then he could hear running footsteps on the wet ground, and they moved back into the forest. He loosened his handgun in its webbing holster. It was Tod and Ian.

Mickey did some quick thinking. 'Look, these blokes are probably from the inner city,' he said. 'Once they're off course they're going to be pretty much lost in the bush in the dark. From where they stopped they'll probably head downhill to the track. Now if it gets to the point they start looking for you they'll move down towards the river. It's easier going. They won't even know they've made the choice. If you take Jacqui through the heavier bush on the high ground you'll be safe.'

Seeing them off, Mickey faded into the forest. What now?

Georgia and Angel heard the men coming a mile off. They were swearing at the bush around them.

154

'Jesus, I don't know what's supposed to be going on here. Why the hell couldn't we drive right in? Where's that fuckin' tree?' complained one. Mickey had been right. Efficient in the city, they were petulant and lost in the dark bushland. Then they saw them, silhouetted for an instant against the white trunk of a ghost gum. 'There's two,' Angel whispered. He pulled his handgun out and held it down behind him. 'We'll just come at them from behind. There won't be a problem.'

Georgia could think of no other way to slow things down. She saw then they both had chainsaws. They were simply going to cut the tree down. Murderous bastards. Jacqui would be the sacrifice. These men were real killers. She and Angel moved silently through the forest on a parallel path with the two men. 'We need a clearing,' she whispered to Angel, 'so we can see what they're doing with their hands.' She had a horror of chainsaws.

Mickey had been a hunter most of his life. As a child he had hunted and fished with his father. Those had been the only good times they had together. His father should have lived in the country. But that was then, and now Mickey knew he could sense game even with his eyes shut. He knew it wasn't magic, just his mind working on the things it heard and smelled, at a level he wasn't consciously aware of, just knew was real. He changed direction. The night felt totally familiar. He didn't ask himself in which direction he was headed, he just moved. He had only met two other people who worked in this way. You sort of recognised each other anyway; there was a level where you communicated. Sometimes it was just a look. Ridgy certainly had something of this quality.

The feeling when it descended on you as you hunted was almost ecstatic. You didn't have to think about balance over the rough ground, or what you would do when you found your quarry; it was a suspended state. All your actions were smooth, almost predestined. He wondered if there were people who moved this way in the world of influence and power.

Somewhere ahead Georgia and Angel stepped out into a small clearing behind the two men. 'Hold it right there,' Georgia said, her handgun levelled. Angel moved closer. 'Drop those bloody things,' he said. 'Don't bend down,' he ordered. 'Just drop 'em.'

'Bloody coppers,' the small thick-set bloke said. He had a beanie pulled low over his brow. 'We were told you were out of here.'

'We're from a special squad,' Georgia said.

'Yeah, arsehole,' Angel added.

A third man, holding a shotgun, stepped into the clearing behind them. Angel didn't see him, just saw the grins on the faces of their captives, and knew something was wrong.

'OK,' the big man said, casually. 'Drop the handguns. Very slowly.' Georgia was angry with herself. They had suspected three. Why hadn't she waited?

The two city lumberjacks squatted to recover their saws.

Mickey stepped behind the third man so quietly his target was surprised to feel the muzzle of the gun nudged into his neck at the carotid artery. 'Move, and your fucking brains will move all the way to banana land,' Mickey said. Angel and Georgia pounced on their own weapons.

Mickey couldn't restrain himself. He hadn't been going to do anything but change the numbers, but the presence of these three men offended him in a way he hadn't reckoned on. He took a step back and punched hard to the side of the man's jaw. The man's head hit Mickey's knee as he went to the ground. He was about to hit him again when Angel grabbed him. 'Hey, Mickey, take it easy.'

They herded them together on the ground, and Georgia kept her gun levelled on them. They didn't seem inclined to play up. But they weren't looking particularly worried, either.

Mickey was finished with his delinquency. He picked up the shotgun and motioned Angel to one side. 'We'll have to let the bastards go,' Mickey said.

'Come on, Mick. This bloke was about to shoot us,' Angel said.

'Without the force backing us it would never hold up,' Mickey said.

Georgia laughed suddenly. 'Let's take them down and chain them around the tree,' she said. 'Let them try and convince the uniformed boys they're not protesters.'

'Aah, I think things are about to get out of hand here, but I like it,' Angel said.

Mickey was uneasy with the smugness of the captives. 'I'd like to put chains around them, all right,' he said, 'and put them to sleep on the river bed.' He sensed something was wrong though. There was something else in the night air.

But the tree seemed to be an appropriate rallying place, and they began to move the three men down the slope and along the road.

Mickey recognised the whine of one of the squad's four-wheel drive vehicles, and he turned to watch it as it came over the rise. Its battery of lights hit the foliage overhead, and then turned their track to the tree to daylight. Mickey thought, well I asked for this, and here it is. I nearly killed that bastard as it was. So I understand what that tempation is about. I'm sure as hell guilty of something. I can't complain. Nevertheless, he caught himself wondering who it was. Hell, he thought, why should I be anxious?

'Now we're really in the shit,' Angel whispered to him.

Whoever was driving didn't lower the lights, and kept their distance. Mickey began to laugh to himself. Whoever it was could only be playing with them. A senior man in an operation like this would rush up and take control.

'It'll be Frog or Sootie,' he said to Georgia. 'Don't worry.'

'I am worried. What have we got ourselves into here?'

Gradually the vehicle drew level with them.

'G'day,' Ridgy said. 'Who are these reprobates?'

'They were about to cut the tree down,' Mickey replied, moving over to Ridgy's window. 'This big bastard held us up with a shotgun. I'd say they were hired to see the tree woman dead. What are you doing up here?'

'Well, when Adams had a think about all the ramifications of this little do, he came down on your side. Unusual that. Anyway, he started telling Sam what a great dad he had, and Sam told him what he thought you were doing. Off trying to save another life. So Frog and I were detailed to rescue you.'

'I don't believe it,' Mickey said.

'Yeah, well that's about as far as it goes. We look after you, and Adams has one of his old mates leak to the papers about the inconsistencies in government contracts for this job. You can't push it any further, Mick. If there's another honest bloke around who sees what's going on, maybe a few other things will take off, but I wouldn't hold my breath.'

'And what do we do with these sods?'

'Arrest them for conspiracy to murder, something like that.'

Ridgy had been doing a lot of thinking on the drive up. Mickey's pushing over this action had finally paid off in a most unexpected way. He'd run rapidly through his own attitude to all this. Was there anything he had to justify to anyone? Personally, he had been backing him, but he also wanted to save Mickey's position on the team, and had thought diplomacy was the only way.

Gina had argued in favour of his supporting Mickey, because he was a friend who was doing the right thing. He had argued back that he knew what was best for Mickey, that Mickey wasn't capable of taking on the darker forces of the city. Gina had said that if everyone did what small thing they could to make it hard for corruption, they'd win in the end. She told him her band refused gigs at bars where hard drugs were sold. 'It doesn't mean much,' she said. 'They probably sell them at most of the bars we play at anyway. But if we find out about it, we don't go there again, and we tell them why. We've even got a song that lays down exactly what crud dope can be, what it can turn innocent kids into.'

Ridgy had felt, as he always did with Gina, insecure in his traditional behaviour. The two people he was most relying on in this time of his life were teaching him something. Nothing was static, everything changed, and finally, it all remained up to individuals acting on their choices, following through. He was smiling as he watched Mickey, Georgia and Angel handcuff the three villains.

After the prisoners were loaded Georgia looked around to find Mickey. He had gone. The idiot bastard, she thought. He's onto something and he's hared off to do the heroics alone. She told the others her suspicion, and Angel was keen to follow him, but Ridgy was having none of that. They settled in for the wait.

Mickey was travelling at a lope through the forest. He would find the vehicle these bastards came in. The bloke carrying the shotgun had been too smug, as if someone else was out there in the forest, someone he imagined could deal with the deep shit they were in.

The night was chillier now, there was a fine mist in the air. He made little sound on the forest blanket, and he knew his eyes were better than most in the dark. The handgun was poked into the back of his belt. Anywhere else would have unbalanced him. He knew his eyes could identify shapes and shadows unerringly. The slightest shape out of place in the forest would draw his eyes. That's how it worked.

He caught sight of the Range Rover just off the track up from the bay. For ten minutes he stood motionless beside a tree, watching. His ears were flat against his head, moved there by involuntary muscle that appeared to act when all-round hearing was required. His breathing slowed so that it was almost non-existent. He made no sound that could disturb his work of sensing the movement of another person.

Wild sound broke through the forest. The occupant of the vehicle had clicked home a tape. The bastard was bored. Careless. Too confident.

Mickey moved around to the rear of the vehicle, checking to see if he had any further worries. He looked through the rear window to check out the contents of the wagon. Nothing. He moved to the rear side window and studied his mark from half a metre away. Prosser!

He took out his handgun and tapped it against the window close to Prosser's ear. He grinned at the shock on the man's face. He has to be stupid, Mickey thought, as he dragged the door open and confronted him. What was he doing making himself legally vulnerable on an operation like this?

Prosser had mental resources though. Not that they were going to do him any good. 'What the hell do you think you're doing?' Prosser asked.

'No, no, no,' Mickey said, tapping the man's chest with the muzzle of the handgun. 'What are you doing here?'

'I'm up here camping,' Prosser said. The man's face was thickly featured. The lips, the eyelids, the nose,

161

were all puffy, in the style of a prize fighter who has taken a lot of beatings. Only Prosser had never stepped into a boxing ring.

'All right, if you're camping,' Mickey said, 'how about some billy tea? Could you spare a cup?'

'Get stuffed,' Prosser said.

'No,' Mickey said, feeling cool in a situation which usually had him running hot. 'It's the other way around.'

'I'll sue you,' Prosser said.

'I don't think so,' Mickey said. 'But if you don't pull out of this, you're going to have some very bad moments in your fucking future, shithead.' He stared into Prosser's eyes, letting the bastard see what strength lay there. Prosser would know any trouble now would be dangerous for him.

'Now,' Mickey added, 'I want a lend of your vehicle to get back to mine. You'll be able to find your way down to the protest area, I think. I saw you up here the other day.

'But before I go,' Mickey said, grabbing Prosser and hauling him from his seat. 'I want to tell you that a lot of coppers are going to be down on you. Your boys were going to shoot my mates down there. Now I don't care who your friends are on the force, they won't be able to overcome that basic feeling of hatred for you, because you threatened other coppers. That's how coppers are, mate. They protect each other. I mean, if the shit started flying, where would it stop?'

Mickey pushed Prosser to the ground, slipped into the driver's seat, and headed down the track to where he hoped Georgia was waiting. Otherwise he was going to have to take the vehicle back to the city and fill out a report. The way things were, there was nothing on Prosser. He would simply deny everything, say he had been up to look at his developments. Couldn't he do that? Yeah, and he was thinking of camping up there, so what was the problem?

Eleven

The woman opened the door to Mickey, Sam and the puppy.

'Donald,' she called back into the house. 'They've bought him. I'm so sorry, Sergeant, I do apologise. We left my nephew in charge of the shop. We knew he was hopeless, but—' She bent down to the pup. 'Oh, he's grown.'

'I fed him pretty well,' Sam said.

'You did a very good job,' she smiled down at Sam. 'You can come and visit him sometime, if you like.'

Mickey smiled at the woman and touched Sam on the shoulder. 'Come on, Sam. See you,' he added to the woman.

'Thanks again Sergeant.'

On the street Mickey looked down at Sam. He was trying to stop his face crumpling into tears.

'You all right, tiger?' he asked.

'Yeah,' Sam said, the tears running silently down his cheeks. 'He was a good dog.'

'Look Sam,' Mickey said. 'I'll talk to Mum about a dog, all right? Maybe she'll get you one.'

'Hey,' Sam said dancing in front of him. 'Thanks, Dad.'

'Hold it. That's a maybe, just a maybe. But if you did get a dog, what sort would you get?'

Sam ran in front of Mickey to the car. He was laughing happily.

That night Mickey watched the television news with Sam. A nice whitewash job had been done on the circumstances surrounding the valley development, but at least something had happened.

The newsreader seemed pleased about the event too, Mickey thought. But then, that could be a newsreader's trick.

'The lone protester, Jacqueline Napier, who spent eight days on the tiny platform, was taken into custody, but later released without charge.' The newsreader appeared to smirk.

Mickey laughed out loud to hear Burke, the press secretary, having to eat it: 'The Premier has full confidence in the police's handling of this protest. The Police Rescue squad in particular showed restraint and responsibility.'

'And what about the development you were on record as being so fervently in favour of?' the television reporter asked.

'Yes,' Burke replied. 'As for the halt on the development, a disturbing number of irregularities have been found in the developer's contract. The government will be looking into these.'

Ah, Mickey thought, it isn't over yet. It'll be back in another guise. I just hope there's another Jacqui about when it happens. And another one of me.

Sam pushed his father's shoulder after the news item had finished. 'You were right,' he said. 'And you know what? I reckon your boss thinks the same thing.'

'The real problem Sam,' Mickey tried to explain. 'Is that you've got to try and be right every bloody day. And that's impossible for me. I don't seem to have time to think about everything. I wouldn't have thought about the forest, or the bay, but for Jacqui climbing that tree.'

Also available from Mandarin

Ellis Weiner

NORTHERN EXPOSURE

Letters from the back of beyond . . .

Halfway between the end of the line and the
middle of nowhere, Cicely is the small Alaskan
town where the young and recently qualified
Dr Joel Fleischman has come – a place which
cannot sleep . . .

Blinking and bewildered, Joel meets Maggie
O'Connell, his beautiful landlady/pilot;
Maurice Minnifield, the ex-astronaut with a
taste for musicals; Ed Chigliak, the Indian with
an IQ that goes off the scale; sixty-two year-old
Holling Vincoeur and Shelly, his shapely young
girlfriend; Chris Stevens, Cicely's metaphysical
DJ; Marilyn Whirlwind, Joel's unshakeable
assistant, and many more. After three months
of sleepless nights, tensions rise and weird
things happen: with *Letters from Cicely*, news
from America's farthest-flung frontier has at
last reached the outside world.

Arthur Daley

STRAIGHT UP

The life story of a legendary Englishman

Arthur Daley is one of Britain's most
distinguished entrepreneurs, a gifted – if
occasionally misunderstood – professional of
the self-made mould. Here, he talks frankly
about his childhood, his early business
initiatives, his time in uniform. He offers
tantalising glimpses of his life with 'Er indoors,
and dwells in some detail on his relationship
with Terry McCann who is no longer in his
employment.

Packed with dazzling escapades and acounts of
his dealings with well known establishment
figures, shot through with unique business
acumen and underpinned with some solid
gold guarantees, Arthur Daley takes full
advantage of his opportunity to set the record
straight. Here, at last, his legion of admirers
have nothing short of the varnished truth.

Straight up.

Frances Fyfield

A QUESTION OF GUILT

When rich, middle-aged widow Eileen
Cartwright becomes obsessed with Michael
Bernard, her handsome solicitor, she plots the
murder of his pretty wife.

A Polish hospital porter is hired for the killing.
Bumbling and remorseful, he is quickly caught.
But Eileen's involvement is harder to prove as
her wealth and cunningly meticulous planning
have put her almost beyond the law. Helen
West and Geoffrey Bailey are the crown
prosecutor and detective superintendent
assigned to the case. Both survivors of personal
trauma, they are drawn together by a weary,
shared compassion.

Only when Eileen Cartwright's extraordinary
evil reaches out even from behind prison bars,
and her unholy alliance with a young
psychopath is revealed, are events brought to a
tense and thrilling climax of frightening and
frenzied violence.

Lynda LaPlante

FRAMED

Lawrence Jackson and Eddie Myers could not
be more different. One is an ambitious young
police officer; the other an escaped supergrass,
now presumed dead. But as Jackson is
staggered to discover when he takes the wife
and kids on holiday in Spain, Eddie Myers is
very much alive.

Extradited back home after an immense
Scotland Yard operation, Myers insists that
Jackson become his chief contact in the
interrogation to follow. The deadly charisma of
one man and the dogged determination of the
other combine to forge a strong bond between
them. But their friendship can only lead to the
most fateful consequences – expecially when a
bank robbery is in the offing . . .

A List of Film and TV Tie-In Titles Available from Mandarin

While every effort is made to keep prices low, it is sometimes necessary to increase prices at short notice. Mandarin Paperbacks reserves the right to show new retail prices on covers which may differ from those previously advertised in the text or elsewhere.

The prices shown below were correct at the time of going to press.

☐	7493 0942 3	**The Silence of the Lambs**	Thomas Harris	£4.99
☐	7493 1416 8	**Wayne's World**	Myers & Ruzan	£4.99
☐	7493 1416 8	**Batman Returns**	Craig Shaw Gardner	£3.99
☐	7493 3601 3	**Rush**	Kim Wozencraft	£3.99
☐	7493 9801 9	**The Commitments**	Roddy Doyle	£4.99
☐	7493 1334 X	**Northern Exposure**	Ellis Weiner	£3.99
☐	7493 0626 2	**Murder Squad**	Tate & Wyre	£4.99
☐	7493 0277 1	**The Bill (Volume 1)**	John Burke	£3.50
☐	7493 0278 X	**The Bill (Volume 2)**	John Burke	£3.50
☐	7493 0002 7	**The Bill (Volume 3)**	John Burke	£3.50
☐	7493 0374 3	**The Bill (Volume 4)**	John Burke	£2.99
☐	7493 0842 7	**The Bill (Volume 5)**	John Burke	£3.50
☐	7493 1178 9	**The Bill (Volume 6)**	John Burke	£3.50

All these books are available at your bookshop or newsagent, or can be ordered direct from the publisher. Just tick the titles you want and fill in the form below.

Mandarin Paperbacks, Cash Sales Department, PO Box 11, Falmouth, Cornwall TR10 9EN.

Please send cheque or postal order, no currency, for purchase price quoted and allow the following for postage and packing:

UK including BFPO £1.00 for the first book, 50p for the second and 30p for each additional book ordered to a maximum charge of £3.00.

Overseas including Eire £2 for the first book, £1.00 for the second and 50p for each additional book thereafter.

NAME (Block letters) ....

ADDRESS ....

....

☐ I enclose my remittance for ....

☐ I wish to pay by Access/Visa Card Number

Expiry Date